DEADLY ARTS
Elizabeth Wetzel

Genevieve Galway is not looking for trouble. She is teaching English at St. Philomena's High School, playing gin rummy, minding her own business.

Then Mark Duchat, a nasty art critic for the local paper, is found murdered at the Cromwell Gallery. And the primary suspect is Traci Beaupré, a young artist and teacher at St. Phil's.

Convinced that Traci is innocent, Gen easily assembles a list of other suspects. Duchat had a talent for offending people—from local artists Clint Madison and Omega Starlight to Traci's former boyfriend, Donald Tomcyk. Gen's unlikely ally in her investigations is Sister Madonna, famous both for her matchmaking and rule-bending.

By the time Gen and Sister Madonna have put the picture together, another victim falls, and Gen appears to be next on the list.

DEADLY ARTS

•

Elizabeth Wetzel

AVALON BOOKS
THOMAS BOUREGY AND COMPANY, INC.
401 LAFAYETTE STREET
NEW YORK, NEW YORK 10003

PRINTED IN THE UNITED STATES OF AMERICA
ON ACID-FREE PAPER
BY HADDON CRAFTSMEN, BLOOMSBURG, PENNSYLVANIA

To my husband, John, who so often claims to be mystified by me that I finally realized the mystery field is where I belong.

Chapter One

"Well, I never have liked him," Ellen said. "He's too good-looking." She discarded the eight of clubs.

"Always a bad sign," I said, picking up the eight.

"Saving eights, hmmm?" she mused, drumming her fingers on the scarred tabletop. "Yes, he reminds me of Gorgeous Glenn." Gorgeous Glenn is Ellen's ex-husband, to whom she was married for eleven long years. Unfortunately, Glenn was never able to give up dating, and Ellen eventually got cranky about it.

"And he's too sophisticated for Traci," I said. "She's only twenty-four, and naive to boot. Gin," I added, spreading my cards and leaning back in the booth.

"Oh, phooey!" She glared at the cards. "I swear you cheat, Gen."

"Quit whining. You owe me—um—$7,281 now. Soon I'll be able to get a new car."

Ellen sighed. "Anyway, Sister Madonna is pretty annoyed about the whole thing, too. It really upset her applecart."

"I know. Poor Madonna. Bad enough that she can't do anything about you and me."

Sister Madonna is the principal of St. Philomena's, the girls high school where Ellen Hudson and I teach. She is the picture of dignity and decorum, and under her prim blue jacket beats the heart of Barbara Cartland. Madonna's patron saint is Noah, and she will not rest until she has us all matched up with the mate of our dreams. Ellen's divorced status is a source of regret, since she can't officially pro-

1

mote a rematch. As for me, there aren't any satisfactory matches on Madonna's list for a fifty-two-year-old widow. Yet.

When she hired Donald Tomcyk to teach science and phys ed last year, it was clear to longtime Madonna-watchers that she saw him happily paired with Traci Beaupré, who teaches French and art. And it looked promising, until Mark Duchat came along in January. Duchat was the art critic for the Derry *Sentinel*, and Traci, besides teaching, was an artist who was developing a following. They had met at the Cromwell Gallery, where her work was being shown.

Adam returned from the bar, carrying mugs of beer, and sat beside me.

"So what do you think, Adam?" I asked, picking up the conversation we had been having before he went to fetch the beer.

He shook his head. "I don't know. Just from what you saw, it's hard to know if there's a problem. After all, you don't like the guy to begin with."

"Agreed," I said. "But she was crying."

I had seen Mark and Traci the evening before, in front of Traci's apartment. Mark grabbed her arm, hard enough to make her cry out. When he saw me, he let her go, and Traci, bursting into tears, ran into the house.

"Ah, Genevieve," he had said, smooth as cream. "How nice to see you again. And looking charming, as always."

I wondered if anything ever flustered the man. His dark eyes were guileless, the smile on his matinée-idol face free of any hint of embarrassment. Mark Duchat was about forty years old, tall and slim, and always impeccably groomed. Too good-looking, as Ellen said.

Ignoring the pleasantries, I cut our interview as short as possible, given that I wasn't called on to be completely rude to Traci's friends. I went inside and tapped at Traci's door. It took her a few minutes to answer, and she wore a smile at odds with her reddened eyes. Everything was fine, she insisted; she had just been upset with Mark. Just a silly quarrel. She didn't seem inclined to invite me in for a chat, so I had had to leave things as they were.

"I know something was wrong," I told Adam.

"But she's not complaining," Adam reminded me. "You said she was fine today."

"But . . ."

"People lose their tempers, Gen. He didn't hit her, just grabbed her arm. Maybe he didn't realize he was hurting her."

"Maybe," I said, unconvinced.

"You can look him over at the art show, Adam," Ellen said.

"Art show?" Adam looked as alarmed as if she had suggested that he join us for a jump into a pit full of vipers.

"Oh, come on, Adam," I said. "Be brave. Lots of people go to art shows and survive. It's for a good cause, after all."

This year Traci had charmed Sharon Cromwell into having a show at the gallery for her senior art students' work, as well as her own. St. Phil's was quite excited, since our exhibits were customarily held in the school gym, and the only patrons were teachers and parents. At the gallery, there was at least the chance that the work might be seen by a passing stranger.

He scowled. "When is this thing?"

"Friday," I said. "And don't tell me you're busy, Mr. Sowinski, because you already told me you're taking a couple days off while the new computers are being installed."

"We have to get your opinion," Ellen said. "As an unbiased observer. We already hate the guy, so we could be wrong, although that isn't at all likely."

Adam sighed and started to shuffle the cards as Ellen slid out of the booth.

"I have to go," she said. "Papers to grade. Watch her, Adam, she cheats."

The bar was emptying; nine o'clock on a Wednesday

night pretty much closes the place. Henry's Hideaway is an old-fashioned neighborhood tavern of worn plank floor, high-backed wooden booths, and a bar presided over by either Henry himself or his wife, Belva. It used to be a hangout for the kids from Derry College back in the days when college students looked for a quiet place where they'd let you make a pitcher of beer last for two hours while you indulged in earnest philosophical discussions. Henry had declined to change with the times, so there was still no loud music, no games, no fancy decor; the only concession to current dogma was that the menu carried the likes of turkey or tuna sandwiches, in addition to the burgers and corned beef that any normal person would prefer. It fits in with the other small shops and businesses that line Division Street in the old section that's my favorite part of the city.

After Brian's death, when I couldn't stand living in our house alone, when I moved to an apartment here in Derry, the Hideaway was a place to go, away from the silence of the apartment, with the friends I needed to be with, where no one demanded false cheer. Two years later, it's as comfortable and familiar as the sofa in front of our fireplace used to be.

We finished off the pitcher and called it a night. Adam walked with me to my apartment two blocks south, and we sat for a few minutes on the wide front steps, enjoying the touch of spring, rare for a March evening in northeast Ohio.

"So, how about a movie Saturday night?" Adam stood up and stretched.

"Um—sure," I said, feeling a little awkward as I always did in such circumstances. I liked Adam, liked him quite a bit, as a matter of fact. The only trouble was—he wasn't Brian. Going out with Adam on what had all the earmarks of a date made me feel as if I were not being quite fair to him. He was an attractive man, after all, and his wife had died eight years before. A lot of women would be only too happy to have his attentions. Still, Adam knew I wasn't ready to even think about a relationship beyond friendship.

He had been Brian's friend, too. "If you survive the art show."

He groaned. "Oh, yeah. So I'll see you then." With a quick wave, he turned and loped down the walk.

My apartment is on the second floor of a beautiful old brick mansion, now converted into six suites with endearingly odd features—small nooks and crannies, a clawfooted tub, flowerlike fixtures where gaslights once hung. There is an elevator now, but climbing the stairs makes me feel virtuous. I shut the door, stepped out of my shoes, and opened the windows to let a bit of spring air into the apartment. The red light glowed on the answering machine, and I rewound the tape and started the playback while I gathered my paperwork.

"Mother, it's Nora. I never seem to get you at home. So would you call and let me know if you'll come during spring break? Robin's just about forgotten she has a grandmother. So call, okay?"

My darling daughter had the slightly aggrieved tone down pat, after much practice. Why was I never home, a woman of my age? Why was I neglecting my only granddaughter? The truth is that Nora always has the faint suspicion that I might be having more fun than is appropriate for me, and, further, that I might be having some of it with her younger sister. Annie is almost as annoying to Nora as I am, still single at the age of twenty-six, making a living of sorts as a photojournalist, living in New York, which everyone knew is a dangerous, dirty, and totally weird place. Nora, on the other hand, is a medical technician, and lives in a Chicago suburb with her sane and sensible accountant husband, Rick, and their seven-year-old daughter. Her unspoken opinion is that the world would be a better place if we would all follow her example.

The tape wound through a message from Polly Fresno about a theater rehearsal, two hang-ups, and a call from the repair shop saying that my VCR was ready. I was half listening, riffling through the essays in my folder.

"Geneviève?" It sounded like "Zhan-vee-ev," the French pronunciation of my name. Only one person says it that way, and my attention snapped back to the tape. There was a long pause before she continued. "It's Traci. I think I am in trouble, Geneviève. I don't know what to do. Please, will you call me as soon as you can?" Her voice ended with a little hiccup, as if she had been crying.

It was the last message. I shut off the machine and dialed Traci's number, already fastening on Mark Duchat as the cause of whatever trouble she had.

There was a busy signal. I tried the number several times before Traci answered.

"It's Gen, Traci," I said. "What can I do for you?"

After a long pause, she said, "Oh, Geneviève. Thank you so much for calling. But—it is no matter."

I frowned at the receiver. "Are you sure? You know I'd be glad to help anyway I can."

"Thank you, Geneviève. But I am all right. I am so sorry to have bothered you."

"No bother," I said. "See you tomorrow, then."

I hung up and kept frowning at the phone. Traci Beaupré grew up in France, with a French father and an American mother, and she is enviably bilingual. But when she is upset she tends to speak English like a textbook. It might not be so noticeable to everyone, but to one who spends her days teaching English to all-American teenagers, it's hard to miss. From what I had just heard, something was definitely wrong.

Chapter Two

The next morning Traci seemed a little subdued, but she smiled when we met in the halls of ivy, and once again assured me that everything was fine. Short of ordering a lie detector test for her, there seemed nothing I could do about it, so I gave up and went off to my daily battle against the forces of illiteracy.

Sister Madonna was at her doorway, keeping watch over the incoming scholars, and when she spied me she beckoned me over and drew me into the office.

"I wanted to ask you about Miss Beaupré." She hesitated. "You are close to her, Mrs. Galway. Is there anything wrong, do you know? I don't want to pry, but I've been a bit concerned."

I shook my head. "Nothing that she's told me, Sister. What have you noticed?"

"I don't know that I can say, exactly. She just doesn't seem to be herself. She is such an enthusiastic young woman, you know. So buoyant. Until recently, that is. Yesterday I asked her for some information about the art show, and she seemed for a moment to have forgotten about it. And I had a strong impression that she had been crying. She assured me that everything is fine, but . . ."

I nodded. "I get the same response, Sister. The only thing I can think of is that she seems to be having problems with her new boyfriend."

"Ah!" That brightened her face right away, of course. "Well, that could explain it. These things are hard for young people. But of course, one recovers and goes on.

Especially when the person involved was really quite un-
suitable.''

I could read her mind: The name ''Donald Tomcyk'' was
emblazoned there, embroidered with little hearts.

''Sister, Sister!'' I wagged my finger at her. ''Are you
at it again?''

''I don't know what you mean, Mrs. Galway. Now I
have a great deal of work to do, so . . .'' But she couldn't
control the telltale blush or the little dimple as she busily
shuffled papers.

I decided against telling her about the argument I had
witnessed between Traci and Mark Duchat. Sister M. tries
valiantly to be charitable, and Mark Duchat was already
straining her resources by interfering with her plans for
Traci.

Traci Beaupré is one of the rare and fortunate young
women whom it is impossible to overlook or to dislike. For
starters, she is a pleasure to look at, a sunshiny blonde with
violet eyes and a smile that lights up the ancient hallways
of St. Philomena's.

It's a source of frustration to the St. Phillies that she is
also sweet and charming, because they would very much
like to hate her for, first, attracting the romantic attentions
of Mr. Tomcyk, with whom most of the Phillies were
madly in love, and, second, dumping said Mr. Tomcyk,
thereby breaking his heart.

It had been the talk of the sophomore class since the
beginning of the second semester, feminism having done
nothing that we could see to distract fifteen-year-olds from
an obsession with romance. Scientists and politicians and
philosophers they may be in due time, but that does not
keep their hearts from going pit-a-pat at the sight of tousled
brown hair and soulful brown eyes and an undeniably
healthy male physique, even if the owner of these features
demands enormous amounts of work in science classes.

Consequently, I made a habit of entering my sophomore
American Lit class with a forbidding frown, so that they

would by no means believe I had any interest in romance, unrequited or otherwise, and had no opinion as to why anyone would be so cruel as to break Mr. Tomcyk's heart.

They glanced up with a sigh when I entered, trailing my dark cloud of repression, and turned their reluctant attention to Willa Cather. We had hardly developed a relationship with Willa when the door opened and Sarah Joplin, the school secretary, came in with a message from Sister Madonna: Would I be willing to help deliver some of the girls' artwork to the gallery after school? Mr. Tomcyk would drive one of the vans, but another was needed and Miss Beaupré had a conference with a parent after school.

I sent her back with an affirmative for Sister and turned back to Willa.

"Mrs. Galway?"

It was not unheard of, but definitely unusual, for Jean Ann Abernathy to join classroom discussion, and I seized the opportunity to call on her.

"Mrs. Galway, don't you think she always looks kind of sad?"

"Who looks sad?" I made a quick search through my memory of *My Ántonia*.

"Miss Joplin," Jean Ann said. "We were just saying, you know, she always looks like—like . . ."

"Sad," Bridget Maguire said.

"Yes," Jean Ann continued. "Don't you think so, Mrs. Galway? I mean . . ."

I narrowed my eyes at her. "Why would Miss Joplin's appearance be of concern to us? Especially when we should be thinking of how sad some of us will look when our next grade card goes home. If we don't exert ourselves to learn about people such as Willa Cather, that is, instead of about people who have a right to a private life, even given their employment in a gossip factory."

Jean Ann favored me with a magnificent sigh and we all concentrated on *My Ántonia*.

It was true, though: Sarah Joplin did always look, if not

sad, at least somber. It wasn't the first time I had thought so, and I had several times intended to invite her over for dinner, include her in one of our shopping forays, something. I hadn't done it yet, though. One of my sins of omission; at this rate I was never going to get into the ranks of even the lesser saints. Next week, I promised myself, I would plan something to include Sarah.

After the last bell, Donald and I loaded the vans with paintings and sculptures and drove to Cromwell Gallery. A young woman seated at the small desk near the side gallery peered at us timidly from beneath beige bangs as we approached. I told her who we were, and she bobbed her head and stood.

"Oh. Oh, yes. Ms. Cromwell said . . ." Her breathy, little-girl voice trailed off, and she cleared her throat and started again. "Ms. Cromwell will be back in just a moment. I'm her—I'm Mary Smith, Ms. Cromwell's assistant. You can—well, I can show you where to bring things in?"

It sounded like a question, so I nodded and she led us to the delivery entrance, where the doorman met us and helped with the unloading. By the time we had everything in, Mary had vanished, and we surveyed the paintings while we waited for Sharon Cromwell to arrive.

"They really did some good things, didn't they?" I asked as we brought the last of the items in.

Donald Tomcyk set a windmillish sculpture on a table and stood looking at it. He looked so forlorn that I had to restrain myself from giving him a hug and patting his tousled head. His hair flopped over his forehead, and his eyes, behind the horn rims, reminded me of a cocker spaniel I had once owned.

"Oh . . . yeah. Yeah, some of the kids are pretty good." He made an effort, smiled, and nodded at a pen-and-ink drawing of a lighthouse with a snake wrapped around its base. "Some of them make you wonder what they're thinking, don't they?"

I laughed. "I always wonder . . ."

An angry voice erupted from the next room. "Listen, you pompous jerk . . ."

Another voice, lower pitched, words indistinguishable, interrupted, and then the first one again, closer.

"Your opinion! You know what your opinion's worth, you cockroach?"

The two men came through the doorway, and I felt Donald tense beside me as I recognized Mark Duchat, Traci's new amour, at the moment wearing a mocking expression.

The other combatant was big and menacing, in his thirties, I guessed. A well-used face, dark hair in a ponytail. I would not have wanted him angry at me, but Duchat didn't seem to be fazed.

"My opinion means a lot to the right people," he said. "After all, isn't that what's got you all lathered up?"

"I wouldn't give two cents for your opinion! What I care about is that you use your lousy column to get even with—"

"Oh, get a grip on yourself, Madison!" Duchat smirked and raised an eyebrow. "Get even? With you? I wouldn't waste a thought on you, let alone column space."

The big man clenched his fists. "Someday someone's going to shut that big mouth of yours, Duchat. Shut it for good."

"Please!" Sharon Cromwell had emerged from the hallway leading to her office. She hurried across the room, her hand raised. "Stop it, both of you! This isn't the place for your arguments."

Duchat shrugged, stood with his hands in his pockets, an amused look on his face, as Sharon and Madison hissed and growled at each other. Finally Madison stalked back into the other room, and Sharon turned to Duchat.

"Why are you here?" Her voice was low, but carrying.

Duchat shrugged. "I needed to talk to you. Didn't Victor call you?"

"No. Well, go into the office. I'm warning you, Mark, I won't put up with . . ." She glanced in our direction, said something in an undertone, and Duchat sauntered into the hallway.

Sharon came over to us. "Sorry about the disturbance. The artistic temperament!" She laughed.

"Oh?" Duchat was a critic, I knew. The other man didn't fit my stereotype of "artist" at all.

"Clint Madison. He's a little upset with Mr. Duchat's review of his work. Now let's see what you've brought me. Will Traci be along soon?"

I explained Traci's delay, and Donald and I exited. The taste of spring that had tantalized us the day before had been replaced by a sharp wind and a snow-sleet mixture that reminded us it was still March. Donald looked as gloomy as the weather, very much as if he would like to assist in shutting Duchat's mouth.

Chapter Three

When I went into the faculty lounge on Friday morning, Donald was having an earnest, though inaudible, conversation with Traci, who kept shaking her head. Sarah Joplin was making tea for herself and Sister Madonna, glancing from time to time at the oblivious pair.

Ellen and Sister Patricia were at the table, checking assignments for the St. Phil's *Beacon*, for which they were the faculty advisors. I got a cup of coffee and joined them as Traci broke away.

"No, you don't understand!" she said. "I can't . . ." She looked at us, as if startled to find that she and Donald were not alone, then snatched up her folders and rushed out of the room.

Donald plunged his hands into his pockets, sighed, and forced a smile. "Well," he said. "Oh, well." He seemed to be trying to find some more words, and we did our best to help with a flurry of chatter, but he gave up and meandered out of the lounge.

Sarah shook her head. "She'd be better off if she'd dump that guy."

"Who? Donald?" I asked, taken aback.

"No! The other one, who seems to be giving her so much grief."

"Mark Duchat," Ellen said. "I couldn't agree more."

Sarah gave a short laugh. "Amazing how easy it is to fall for rats, isn't it? Oh, well, I guess that's life." She gathered up the teacups and left.

"Sooo," Ellen said. "She left a rat in Chicago. That explains a lot."

Sarah had come to St. Phil's in the fall, and since then the resident gossips had found out little about her private life. She was thirtyish, tall and slender, with shoulder-length ash-blond hair; generally quiet, friendly in a non-chummy way; and, as the Phillies had pointed out, she always seemed just a little sad.

"Ah," I said, "what a world it would be if we had no affaires de coeur. Why do you suppose Sister Madonna hasn't gotten to work on Sarah, by the way?"

"Good grief." Sister Patricia groaned. "We ought to rename this school—St. Valentine's would be more like it."

"And we could offer a Lonelyhearts Club as one of our extracurriculars," I said.

"Now, there's an idea, Pat!" Ellen said. "We could start an advice-to-the-lovelorn column in the *Beacon.*"

"Perfect," I said. "I have a whole class of candidates who would love to write it."

The first bell rang and I went forth to meet, thankfully, the seniors in my English Lit class, who were more interested in their college applications than in the love lives of any of their teachers.

Much to my annoyance, I found that I had to make a major effort to shove my own speculations about Traci into a corner of my mind to make room for Jane Austen. I am not pleased when distractions interfere with teaching, whether my own distractions or the students'. But Traci's woebegone face kept intruding on my thoughts.

Not that I was mesmerized by her romantic woes, since I long ago learned from my daughters that those matters are best left to the principals. What kept nagging at me was the conviction that something other than a rocky romance was at the root of it, that, somehow, Mark Duchat was as sinister as he was good-looking.

And it was none of my business, I reminded myself irritably. Traci Beaupré was a grown woman, responsible for her own life. She was a good teacher. She was an accomplished artist. And if she did need advice, she had a set of parents who were undoubtedly capable of providing same.

The thing was, grown or not, Traci seemed too young and fragile to be on her own, and her parents were in France. In the three years she had been at St. Phil's, she had asked my advice on many matters, and I was happy to give it. Once a mother, always a busybody, I suppose, and my own daughters had never given me half the opportunities I would have liked.

Nora, for instance, had my dark hair and navy-blue eyes, and apparently confused our respective roles early in life. Picture Nora at age four, and me, very pregnant, fulminating about the chaos in her room while she stands patiently listening; the phone rings, and Nora, patting my arm, says, "I'll get the phone, Mom. You need some time out. When I come back, we'll talk." I don't think I ever regained the upper hand.

And Annie, with her father's auburn hair and eyes like October blue skies, got on her feet at age one, took off running, and hasn't stopped since. Annie meets life head-on, and gives no quarter.

Traci was a new experience for me.

However, her problems had receded from my mind by lunchtime, routed by the Macbeths, Bret Harte, and Joyce Carol Oates. I took my lunch and joined Ellen in the lounge.

"Well, how are the plans for a lovelorn column?" I asked.

"Oh, Sister Pat chickened out. For some reason, she thought Madonna might not approve."

"Yes," I said. "Sauce for the goose is definitely not for the goslings." Sister Madonna might be dedicated to matching up any stray adults who came her way, but her hobby did not extend to the students, who, in her opinion, had a long way to go before thinking of such things, a way leading through college and a worthwhile career. If she had her way, all of the Phillies would win Nobels or Pulitzers, or, failing that, at least an Oscar—for a worthwhile film, of course. Then they would marry men who were deserving of them. Not a bad scenario, actually.

"I was running through the microfilms of back copies of the *Sentinel* during my free period," Ellen said. "Thought it might be interesting to find out about Duchat."

"And?"

She sighed. "No criminal record that I could find, darn it. Not a whole lot about him, anyway. When he started at the paper, they did a little bio to introduce him, but just the usual stuff. Worked at a gallery in Pittsburgh, then in New York, then spent a few years in Europe. That was all."

"Shoot," I said. "No mention of wives who disappeared under mysterious circumstances?"

"Nope. But he is one nasty hombre. I looked at a few of his columns. He doesn't often have a word of praise for the poor artists he reviews. Look, I printed out the column on Clint Madison, the artist you saw at the gallery. No wonder he was so mad."

I scanned the printout:

The Cromwell Gallery offers a showing of the works of two local artists this week. The question is, why?

"Ouch," I said.

Clint Madison afflicts us with his usual self-consciously angry scrawls. The so-called artist appears to believe that big is synonymous with great, thus assaulting the senses with enormous canvases filled with vacuity.

He went on to describe, scathingly, some of the individual works, and ended with:

Amusingly enough, word is that the city fathers are about to award Madison a contract to create the focal artwork for the new civic building. Something we can all look forward to seeing on a regular basis, I'm sure.

"Well," I said, "I can see where Mr. Madison might be a teensy bit annoyed."

The other local artist didn't fare any better, I noticed. The column continued:

Adding insult to injury, we find the dabblings of Omega Starlight, whose work is as serious and authentic as her name. Starlight achieved fame of a sort as a performance artist, in which calling she at least brought pain to only a limited number of people, those misguided souls who, apparently deliberately, chose to attend her performances. Now she evidently intends to spread her derivative inanity farther afield.

"My, my, my!" I said. "Is this a charmer, or what?"

"Mr. Sensitivity," Ellen said. "How in heaven's name did Traci get involved with the likes of him?"

"An evil spell?" I guessed. "Hypnotism?"

"Maybe he's a dual personality," Ellen said. "In which case, I suspect the Mr. Hyde part has been showing its face to Traci lately. I don't care what she says; I think she's scared of something."

"Or someone." I nodded. "Well, there's nothing anyone can do about it unless she lets us in on it. Just wait and see."

Chapter Four

"What's this one supposed to be?" Adam frowned at the painting, which depicted an assemblage of what appeared to be sticks and boards at various angles, against a background of clouds.

I read the title card: *Low Tide.*

Adam turned his frown to me. "What tide? Where's the ocean? Where's the beach?"

"You have to use your imagination," I said, trying not to laugh. "Maybe it's the low tide in a person's life, and the sticks are—um—obstacles?"

So far the art exhibit seemed to be living up to Adam's expectations.

"Uh-huh," he said, raising an eyebrow and moving on to the next piece, a charcoal picture of a covered bridge. "Now that has possibilities," he declared.

"My, Adam, you sound like an old hand at this." Ellen materialized beside us, holding a brochure describing the work on display. "You have to admit, some of the kids are really talented."

The gallery was crowded with nervous students, proud parents, bored siblings, and the cheering section from St. Phil's.

"What I want to know is, don't any of them paint anything cheerful?" Adam asked. "You could get a real case of depression if you hung around here a lot."

"You ought to read some of the poetry they write," Ellen said. "After I read a batch of submissions to the *Beacon*, I want to go home and kick the cat. Once we ran

18

a contest for poetry on the topic 'Hope.' You wouldn't believe what that brought forth.''

I laughed. ''Maybe you have to endure the world for a few years before you learn what's worth suffering over. Angst is a privilege of the young.''

We joined Sister Madonna and Sister Patricia, who were standing with Sharon's assistant, Mary Smith, in front of an impressionist watercolor, three prancing horses in a dreamlike landscape.

''Look at this,'' Sister Madonna said, her eyes shining. ''I'd like to have this one. It's exactly what I need for my brother's birthday gift. He would just love it!''

''It's beautiful,'' I agreed.

''They are going to be sold, aren't they?'' she asked. ''How much are they asking for it?''

Mary scanned the brochure. '' 'Number forty-two, *Unfettered*.' Here it is—one hundred twenty-five dollars.''

Sister Madonna tilted her head, examining the picture from different angles, and chewed her lower lip for a few seconds. ''Well, I'm going to get it,'' she decided. ''After all, a person turns fifty just once. And he's my only brother. And it will look perfect in their family room.''

''It's a wonderful painting, Sister,'' Mary said softly. ''Why don't I—well, you see, I have to—I'm afraid I have to leave, but I'll make a note for Ms. Cromwell. That you want the painting, I mean.'' After a few flutters, she drifted away.

Her decision made, Sister Madonna smiled triumphantly and turned her attention to us.

I introduced Adam, and Ellen added, with a small, wicked grin, ''Adam is a good friend of Genevieve's.''

Sister's smile grew larger, and her eyes took on the sparkle that we knew so well. ''Mr. Sowinski, how nice to meet you!'' She shook his hand, flashing her dimples every which way, her eyes shooting a few extra sparkles my way. ''Are you enjoying the exhibit?''

"Yes, Sister," he lied, sounding exactly like a schoolboy.

"Is your family with you, Mr. Sowinski?" Madonna asked, with a perfect blend of casual interest and Christian concern. Certainly no one could accuse her of prying. "Is your wife interested in art?"

Adam looked confused. "I—uh—no, Sister. I mean . . ."

"Mr. Sowinski isn't married, Sister," Ellen said helpfully.

"Ah!"

Sister Pat rolled her eyes, and I gave Sister Madonna a frown, which she repaid with a serene smile. Fortunately, she was not empowered by either the church or the state to declare us man and wife; still, not taking any chances, I insisted on leaving her behind, leading my treacherous friend and the baffled Adam away.

"Oh, well, shoot!" Ellen said. "What's *he* doing here?"

I followed her glare and found Mark Duchat at the end of it. He was talking to Sarah Joplin, and even from across the room it didn't appear that she was enjoying his company. His face wore the same charming veneer he employed on me whenever we met, a veneer beneath which I always sensed contempt for us peasants, and Sarah was regarding him as if he were something disgusting left on her lawn.

"Probably looking for the next victim for his column," I said. "By the way, Adam, that is the charming Mark Duchat we were telling you about. You see how obnoxious he is?"

Adam snorted. "Gen, I can't tell anything about him. All I see is a guy who's probably being a jerk. I admit he's got a look I don't like, and he's probably real full of himself, but I don't know that. And, yeah, I admit that, just on impulse, I think I'd like to punch him in the mouth, but . . ."

"Well, of course you're right to withhold judgment,"

Ellen agreed. ''I admire people who don't jump to conclusions.''

''Yes,'' I said. ''The number of people who are intrigued by the thought of punching Mr. Duchat in the mouth is growing. Soon we'll have to take numbers.''

Sarah turned her back and walked away from Duchat, her face flushed, and joined Donald, who was staring disconsolately at a ceramic bowl full of ceramic fruit.

Duchat slithered toward Traci, and we went to head him off. Traci was nervous as a cat in a fiddle factory tonight as it was, and considering the effect Duchat had on her lately, she didn't need him to bug her.

''Oh, Geneviève!'' she said. ''Ellen, Adam! I'm so glad you came. I need all the encouragement I can get tonight! Do you think the exhibit is doing well?''

''It's wonderful,'' I said. ''You should be so proud of your students.''

''And yourself,'' Ellen said. ''Sister Madonna is buying one of your paintings, the one with the horses.''

''I am flattered,'' she said, her cheeks reddening. ''Sister Madonna is very knowledgeable. I—''

She broke off, and her face changed, tautening. I turned to see Duchat behind me.

''Traci!'' he said. ''Congratulations! Your little show is quite successful.''

''Merci,'' she murmured, her hands twisting her scarf, her eyes darting from side to side as if seeking escape.

I scowled at him. ''Traci, I know Sister Madonna would like to talk to you about that painting,'' I said, taking her arm and propelling her to safe harbor among the nuns.

''Well?'' I asked Adam after we deposited Traci.

He nodded. ''Well, yes. I'd have to agree that it looks like she's afraid of him. But there still isn't anything I can see to do about it. Traci hasn't asked for help, you haven't seen the guy do anything illegal, and it isn't a crime to be disgusting.''

''Well, it ought to be,'' I said. ''People shouldn't be

allowed to run around annoying everyone. We ought to be able to vote on it.''

Someone bumped me from behind.

''Oh, sorry!'' Sarah had backed into me.

''No damage done,'' I said. ''I see you met Mark Duchat. What do you think now?''

She grimaced. ''What on earth does Traci see in him? Aside from the fact that he's an oily creep, he evidently thinks he's God's gift to all women.''

''Ah,'' Ellen said. ''So he was trying to mesmerize you, too.''

Sarah blushed. ''It was that obvious? Well, I'm sure he comes on to every woman he sees.''

''Is that a refreshment table I see?'' Ellen asked. ''Come on, let's get the taste of Duchat out of our mouths.''

Sharon Cromwell offered us coffee and small but dangerous pastries.

''There's punch, if you prefer,'' she said. ''We thought wine might not be appropriate, but . . .''

''No,'' I said. ''Coffee is fine. In fact, this is marvelous.''

She smiled. ''Well, I'm something of an addict, and I love to try special blends. It's hard for anyone to get out of here without my plying them with coffee.''

Several parents came to the table to be plied, and we sipped and munched our way through the exhibits.

''Listen, big shot . . .''

A voice raised just enough to be heard over the murmur of the crowd. Heads turned, whispers stirred.

''Don't try that attitude with me! I'm just going to tell you once more—stay away from her!''

A little knot of people moved away, and we saw Donald, toe-to-toe and nose-to-nose with Mark Duchat.

Duchat gave a short, derisive laugh. ''Oh, really, now! Don't you think that should be up to her?''

''Look, I don't know what you're up to, but you're not

going to do anything to her, understand? You let her alone!''

"Oh, *mon Dieu!*" Traci and Sister Madonna were beside us, Traci's eyes wide and terrified.

"Mr. Tomcyk," Sister said, taking a step toward the men.

I had missed Duchat's reply, but my head swiveled back to the tense twosome as Donald spoke.

"Yes, I will do something about it, Duchat! Whatever it takes!''

Duchat turned away, flicking a dismissive hand at Donald. "Oh, grow up, sonny. Don't make more of a fool of yourself than you already have.''

Donald grabbed his arm and spun him around, his fist coming up, and Traci gasped. Sister Madonna moved forward, but Adam moved faster, covering the distance in three giant steps and getting between Donald and Duchat. He spoke to Donald, his voice inaudible to us, but obviously persuasive, as Donald lowered his fist and allowed himself to be turned away. Duchat, recovering from a momentary surprise, regained his usual smirk and strolled into the adjoining gallery.

Traci came out of her trance and went to Donald, and they melted into the crowd. Gradually people composed themselves and turned their attention to the other exhibit.

"Well," Sister Madonna said. "I did think we were going to have more of a show than we expected. Not exactly what St. Philomena's would want to its credit! Mr. Sowinski, we certainly owe you our thanks for your quick thinking.''

If she had harbored any doubts about Adam before, it was clear that he was now high on her list of picks.

At nine o'clock parents began to shepherd their tired daughters homeward, and soon only our little group remained—Adam, Ellen, Donald, and I, and the nuns. Sister Charlotte, who was driving the nun brigade, was jingling her car keys in a none-too-subtle hint, and Sister Madonna went off to arrange for the purchase of her painting.

Donald, looking a little sheepish, stopped on his way to the door. "Thanks, Adam. Guess I got a little carried away."

"Happens to the best of us." Adam grinned and slapped him on the shoulder.

"A lot of us have had the same urge where Duchat is concerned," Ellen said. "Don't let him get to you."

"Well," I said. "We have done our duty by dear old St. Phil's. I'm out of here as soon as I say good-bye to Traci. Where is she?"

As if summoned by my thought, Traci emerged from the hallway and hurried toward us. Her eyes were feverishly bright, her cheeks red, and I could almost feel the tension emanating from her. Now what?

She smiled a too-bright smile. "So, it is time to blow this peanut gallery, *n'est-ce pas?*"

I joined in the laughter at the slightly off-kilter idiom, but my nerves gave a warning tingle.

"Well, that's settled." Sister Madonna came back. "Miss Cromwell is going to get a receipt for me, and I can pick up my new painting on Monday, after the exhibit ends. Miss Beaupré, I am so delighted with it!"

"Thank you, Sister. I—"

There was a crash from the direction of the gallery office, startling us to silence.

Sharon Cromwell rushed from the hallway, her face a mask of horror.

"Help, oh, help!" she gasped, and Adam strode toward her.

"What is it? What is it, my dear?" Sister Madonna followed Adam.

"He's dead," Sharon said thickly. "He's . . . he's . . ."

"Where?" Adam asked.

She stared at him, raised a shaking hand, and pointed. "In the office. He's . . ."

Adam ran to the hallway and disappeared.

"Who?" I asked. "Who's dead?"

But I knew before Sharon managed to force the words out.

"Mark—Mark Duchat . . . oh, no!"

Without a sound, Traci had crumpled in a heap beside me.

Chapter Five

Nobody had said anything for a long time. The occasion didn't lend itself to small talk and the important details had been imparted pretty quickly.

The police had arrived posthaste—Lieutenant Linda Marino and Sergeant Frank Monroe. I knew both of them, since Brian had been on the force before pulling disability and going on to teach at Derry College. Good cops and good people. They set up shop in a small anteroom, talking to each of us in turn.

For the past hour we had all slouched or slumped like a collection of rag dolls in the side gallery, watching the arrival of investigators and the small group of reporters waiting for a story.

Only Sister Madonna still sat upright, without a sign of either impatience or exhaustion. Something they taught in nun school, no doubt. She and Sisters Patricia and Charlotte were saying their rosaries silently, though Sister Pat showed a tendency to doze off periodically, coming back with a start. They could have gone home after being questioned, but they would never desert the rest of us.

Traci had recovered before the police arrived, and now sat on a bench beside the door to the hallway, her face waxy and expressionless. Donald had given up trying to talk to her, and was leaning against the door frame, looking mopey. Ellen sat across the room, reading the gallery brochure for the tenth time in an increasingly difficult effort to stay awake.

I hoped I looked better than any of them, and then decided that might not be so good considering the position we now found ourselves in. Did you look guiltier, I wondered, if you were pale and catatonic, or if you were rosy and alert? A happy medium would probably be best, I decided, but that appeared to be a state available only to the nuns. Well, of course, probably none of them was afraid of being considered a suspect in a murder, nuns not being particularly noted for such behavior.

At any rate, I had been summoned already, as had Ellen, and our information had surely added nothing to the case. Both Sgt. Monroe and Lt. Marino appeared willing to believe that I knew nothing.

Sharon, though still wan, had regained her composure by the time the police had arrived. She had gone to her office to put Sister Madonna's check in the safe, she said, and had found Mark lying on the floor beside her desk. There was blood on his head. As soon as she touched his arm, she knew he was dead. Now she sat in an armchair near the doorway, staring at the carpet, every so often glancing up at Traci, then quickly away.

Adam had checked for a pulse before calling the police, he said. He saw what he presumed was the weapon, a small, heavy bronze statue. He was in the anteroom now, taking his turn at being interviewed. Since he and Sharon were the only ones who had any information, it must have been a tedious evening for the homicide detectives, too, I supposed. None of us had been back in the office all evening, except for Sharon, who wouldn't likely have murdered anyone in her own office, at least not during an exhibit.

Of course, the hallway that led back to the office also led to the rest rooms, as well as to a smaller gallery and a studio . . .

Unbidden, the picture rose from the corner of my mind where I had stifled it several times in the past hour. Traci coming from the hallway that led to the office—and, I reminded myself yet again, to the rest rooms, the small gallery, the studio! Ignoring my argument, the picture persisted: Traci, flushed and breathless, looking as if her small body might fly into pieces, speaking in Franglais . . . *Don't be ridiculous!* I ordered myself. Lots of people had left the gallery for a few minutes, most of them probably headed for the rest rooms. Even Sister Charlotte had come and gone. Even Donald . . .

Which, come to think of it, did not seem comforting. Could Donald . . . ?

Oh, for heaven's sake! I gave myself a pinch and commanded myself to stop fantasizing. Donald had already been questioned and was still not in handcuffs, even though the police knew about his altercation with Duchat.

Adam came out and slumped into the chair beside me. One of the detectives led Traci back to the hallway. After her, I hoped, we could all go home.

"Any ideas?" I asked. Adam had a lot of friends on the force, having worked with the department as a consultant on a number of computer applications.

"FYI," he said, keeping his voice low. "The statue was pretty likely the weapon, all right. No prints, though; it was wiped clean. But some traces of blood in the crevices."

"Wiped with what?" I asked. "Did they find anything with blood on it?"

He shook his head. "There are a lot of rags in the next room, where they hold classes. All kinds of paint, including plenty of red. They'll all be gone over."

I thought for a minute, trying to remember other things I had learned. "Wouldn't the killer have gotten blood on him? None of us has any stains, so . . ."

"Not necessarily," Adam said. "He was whacked over the head just once. There wasn't a lot of blood."

"So they don't have much to work with?"

"One other thing." He glanced around, but no one else was paying any attention. "Duchat was clutching a scarf. I didn't see it when I checked him out; I guess it was underneath him. One of the guys brought it in while I was talking to Monroe. Couldn't see much, it was in a bag, but it's one of those square silk things, blue, with some kind of design. It isn't the kind of thing I usually notice, but I bet someone will recognize it.''

''I'm sure. A woman's scarf? Funny, I guess I just assumed . . .'' My voice caught as I felt a jolt of memory: Traci's nervous fingers tugging at her scarf, a blue silk scarf with a darker blue geometric pattern.

''What?'' Adam said.

I swallowed hard, shook my head. ''Nothing.''

He eyed me suspiciously, but let it go.

It seemed like forever before Traci came out, and I was relieved to see that she was also unshackled.

Sgt. Monroe followed Traci from the hallway. ''I think we're through here for tonight, folks. You're all free to go. We'll want to see some of you again, so please stay available.''

There was a general stirring, sighs of relief. I looked at Traci and could see nothing but exhaustion. That young woman was not a murderer, I told myself firmly, and I was pretty sure I believed it.

Chapter Six

The phone nagged me awake, which ticks me off on any Saturday morning, never mind a Saturday morning following such a Friday. I cursed briefly and pulled my pillow over my head until the machine picked up.

"Mother? Are you there, Mother?" Nora sounded annoyed, though I couldn't imagine what I might have done now, and I was darned if I'd get out of bed to let her yell at me first thing in the morning.

"It says on the news that a teacher at your school is being questioned about a murder. What's going on? Mother, if you're there, I wish you'd pick up the phone." She paused, evidently waiting for me to do so, of which there was a fat chance. A loud sigh, then, "Well, please call me when you get in."

I sat up and let my feet grope for slippers, since it was clear that sleep had fled. A pox on freedom of the press, and on telephones, for that matter.

As if in spite, the miserable thing rang again, and I stomped across the room, snatched the receiver, and barked, "Hello!"

"Wow!" Annie gasped in mock terror. "Hey, Mom, I didn't do it, honest, and I'll never do it again."

I laughed in spite of myself. "Sorry, dear. It's been a trying time."

"I guess," she said. "I was just hearing about your school being involved in a murder."

"I wish everyone would stop calling it *my* school," I

said. "I have a feeling they're thinking of this as *my* murder, too."

Annie chuckled. "Everyone? Guess that means Nora's called already, huh? Well, after all, Mother dear, they said a teacher was being questioned. And you are a teacher at the designated school. One wants to know if one's mother is likely to be showing up on the evening news."

"One needn't worry," I said, and gave her a brief synopsis.

"Well," she said, "okay. Stay out of trouble, now. I'm going up to Maine on an assignment, and I don't want to come back to any nasty surprises."

After wishing Annie bon voyage, I headed for the kitchen and communed with Mr. Coffee, and while he got to work I returned Nora's call, repeated the story, and assured her that I was not a murderer.

I had just enough time to pour a glass of juice before the phone summoned me again. Deciding that it was time for me to train myself to ignore it, I padded past it with only a sidelong frown, opened the door, and picked up my paper. There was the story, on page one. I scanned it, sipping my juice as I waited for the fifth ring to trigger the answering machine.

"Zhan-vee-ev? This is . . ."

I knew who it was. I lunged for the receiver, slopping juice down the front of my robe.

"Traci? I'm here! Wait—" I shut off the machine, which squealed in protest. "What's wrong?"

"Oh, Geneviève," she said. "I don't know what to do. I am very afraid."

"Why? Have the police been . . ."

"No, not that. At least, not yet. But when the police find out, then maybe they will think more that I did kill Mark. But I would not, even for that. But I think they will not believe me. I don't know what to do."

I shook my head, hoping to clear the cobwebs. "Traci,

dear, you're not making sense. Find out what? What are you talking about?''

She took a long breath. ''Can I come there? I must tell what happened, and maybe you can tell me what I must do. I do not want to bother, but . . .'' There was a little tremor in her voice.

''It isn't a bother,'' I said. ''Come right over. I'll give you breakfast. We have all day. We'll figure it out.''

I hung up and headed for the kitchen, but not fast enough. The phone rang again, with a particularly nasty note of triumph that I've noticed before from time to time. I know when I'm beaten.

''Yes?'' I hissed into the mouthpiece.

''I'm not selling anything,'' Adam assured me. ''Just want to see if you've read the paper.''

''Just got it. What's up?''

''According to 'sources,' Traci seems to be a prime suspect. They don't have enough to charge her, but they supposedly have an eye on her.''

I told him about Traci's call. ''She's coming over to tell me what's wrong. Want to join us?''

''You think she'd be willing to spill it if someone else is there?''

''You're a hero, Adam. She'll trust you as much as she does me. Come over. I'll give you some breakfast, too.''

Then I went to the kitchen, poured a cup of coffee, and wondered what I was going to fix for breakfast. Usually I had cereal (unsweetened) with low-fat milk and a sliced banana, since, like most right-thinking Americans, I have been browbeaten into healthy eating by the Surgeon General and the other assorted nags. This occasion seemed to call for something more.

I decided to tempt the cholesterol demons and make an omelet. Fortunately, I had bought a dozen eggs last week, and so had ten left, since I am permitted to eat them at the rate of two per week. There was a chunk of ham in the freezer, left over from Christmas; I dug it out and put it in the microwave to thaw. Yes! An omelet, complete with ham and cheese. Low-fat cheese, but the thought was there.

Flushed with defiance, I looked around for other culinary sins I might commit. Muffins, I decided. They used to be a specialty of mine in the bad old days. I put on a sweatsuit and tennis shoes, brushed my hair, poured another round of caffeine, and got to work, feeling more optimistic by the minute. A decent hour had finally arrived and sunlight was filling the kitchen, a good sign, I thought.

I had the muffins ready for the oven and the omelet ready for the pan when the doorbell announced the arrival of either the nutrition police or my guests.

It was Adam, with a cantaloupe and a jar of honey. I got him a knife to deal with the melon while I set the table.

"So," I said, "why are they so sure Traci did it? Just because he had her scarf?"

Adam shook his head. "They know she was having some kind of problem with him. I don't know who told them that—probably Sharon, but apparently Traci admitted it. Also, she was back there shortly before Duchat's body was found."

"So were a lot of other people," I said, not for the first time. We had been all through this the night before, hanging out at Henry's Hideaway until well after midnight. Ellen, Adam, and I.

The doorbell signaled Traci's arrival. She looked tired, a little pale, but no longer scared witless. I shooed her into the kitchen, sat her down, and urged melon on her. In between bites she filled us in on her session with the police.

"They ask to know why Mark and I were arguing, because I told them he got my scarf when he grabbed at me."

I slid the omelets onto warm plates and set a basket of muffins on the table. "Eat," I said. "And enjoy it, or else."

"No problem," Adam said. "My compliments to the chef."

"Very delicious, Geneviève," Traci said, smiling for the first time. She dabbed honey on a muffin.

"So," I said. "The police asked about your quarrel?"

She nodded. "I told them I did not want to see him anymore, and he was making difficulties. After a while, they said I can go home, but not to go away from Derry. Because they will want to talk to me more."

"Well," I said, "if they're basing their suspicions on the fact that you argued with Mark, they ought to know that you're not exactly unique in that. From what I've seen so far, practically everyone who knows him has argued with him."

She sighed. "But maybe not just before he was killed, yes? And he has a scarf belonging to no one else."

"Doesn't mean a thing," I said, with a confidence I was far from feeling.

"But there is more," she said. "I have not told the police all. But I don't think I can hide it now. And I am afraid no one will believe the way it was."

Adam and I looked at each other. I wondered whether we wanted to hear this after all. At some point, the police might want to question us again, too.

"That is why I want to tell you," Traci said softly.

"Ooo-kay," I said. I stacked the dishes, poured fresh coffee, and awaited the revelation.

Chapter Seven

"When I was an art student in Paris," Traci said, "one of the practices I did was to copy paintings, and then sometimes to do other paintings in an artist's style. You know, the kind of landscapes Corot did, or Cézanne's bathers. I liked very much the impressionists, like Matisse and Renoir. You know the sort of works I mean?"

Adam tried to look wise, and I nodded. "Some of my favorites, too."

"Well," she said, "some of the pieces I did were liked by people at the school. And people bought them." She sighed and stopped for a moment, then continued. "This is quite all right, you know, to make paintings of certain styles. Also to make copies. It is sometimes how one proceeds when one has not yet made a personal style, you see."

"I've read that," I said. "Why is that a problem?"

Traci shook her head. "It is not, Geneviève. Only if one sells such work as if it were by the famous artist is it a bad thing. And I did not. And my paintings were not old enough to be mistaken for ones that were done a hundred years ago, or even fifty years, of course. Aging makes cracks and other blemishes, you see."

"Yes," I said. "So . . ."

"So," she said. She clasped her hands in her lap, so hard that the knuckles whitened. "So, a dealer named Victor Ingle has bought a number of my paintings. I am very grateful to him, because this money has made my studies much easier, of course. He is an American, and when I say

I am going to come here, he says he knows people here who will like my work.''

I was beginning to get an inkling of what was coming.

''I was happy to meet Sharon Cromwell,'' Traci went on, her voice quavering. ''She was very helpful, she bought a few of my paintings—my own work, you understand, since I was not doing the imitations any longer. And also I met Mark—Mark Duchat, who said so many nice things about my work. He said Victor had told him of the other paintings, and I showed him the ones I had kept. He insisted on buying them. Oh, I was so flattered!'' She made a sound between a laugh and a sob.

''Uh-oh,'' I said, and Adam looked at me and frowned.

''When I went to New York to see my parents for the holidays, I visited the galleries, of course. In one of them was a painting by Corot on exhibit, a painting that was much written of, previously unknown. I was eager to see it.''

She looked at me, her eyes filled with tears. ''But I had seen it before. I knew it was mine at once, even though my signature was no longer there. I had sold it to Victor Ingle two years ago.''

''I don't get it,'' Adam said. ''You said your paintings weren't old enough . . .''

She sighed. ''If you wish to deceive, there are ways to make a painting old, you see, I mean to look old. And Corot—well, Corot is one of the artists most copied, most passed off as originals. Also, he often did not sign his work. So . . .''

''Well, I should think that would make people more likely to question a 'new' painting,'' I said.

''Yes, of course. But then one relies on the provenance, and if that is considered reliable . . .''

''What's a provenance?'' Adam asked.

''Like a pedigree,'' I told him.

''Yes,'' Traci said. ''It is like a history of who has

owned the piece. And then there are documents from experts who say this is genuine. Sometimes they are wrong.''

''A common problem with experts,'' I said. ''So what did you do?''

''I did not know what to do,'' she said. She took out a tissue and wiped her eyes. ''I am afraid I will be accused of a forgery. So I think, I will ask Mark how to make this right. Since he is a respected critic, he will know the right people to talk to, *n'est-ce pas*?''

''Ah, *oui*,'' I said. ''Good old Mark.''

Traci jumped up and began pacing. ''But when I tell him, he laughs at me! He says Victor Ingle is a well-known dealer, and he will say I have tricked him. Then I find that the other paintings that Mark has bought from me he has sold also. He says he will be able to prove that I am the one who has done the illegal things, if I tell about it.''

''How would he prove that?'' Adam asked. ''If you didn't know about it . . .''

''But if documents can be faked to prove a painting is genuine, they can be faked to prove other things, too,'' I said.

Traci nodded, looking miserable. ''And now, I think, if I must tell the police this, they will surely believe I killed Mark because of it.''

''Either because you did it and he was going to turn you in, or because you were mad at him for doing it,'' I said. ''What a mess.''

''Oh, Geneviève!'' She drew a long, tremulous breath. ''I am very afraid. I was in the back rooms at the gallery when we had the show, and Mark was holding my scarf when they found him. It must look very bad for me.''

''Yeah, well, it's sure a lot for the cops to think about,'' Adam said. ''What about the scarf, Traci? How did Duchat come to have it?''

''And why were you in the back rooms?'' I asked.

Traci wiped away a fresh supply of tears. ''I found out that Mark was keeping two of my paintings that he had bought in the studio at Sharon's gallery. I thought, if I could get them—it would not make right what had already been done, but at least I might be able to stop them from doing more. But . . .'' Her voice broke and she covered her eyes with both hands.

''Mark caught you,'' I guessed.

She nodded, struggling for control. ''He must have been watching, and saw me go through the hall. I had just taken a knife and begun to cut the canvas from the frame. But then Mark came in. He was so angry! He grabbed my arm. He said he would tell the police and I would go to prison. I struggled to get away, and the knife cut his arm. He was so surprised, he let me go. I dropped the knife and started to run away, and he reached to catch me again, and that's when he got my scarf. But I got away. And—and that was the last time I saw him.'' Tears were running unheeded by that time, and she huddled in the chair, looking waiflike.

''That was when you came out and joined us?'' I asked, feeling a prickle of alarm. It had been no more than five minutes after Traci came out that Sharon discovered the murder. If the detectives reconstructed events, I doubted that they would buy the proposition that someone else had been lurking, ready to do Duchat in the minute Traci left him.

She shook her head. ''No. Victor was in the small gallery. He asked me what was wrong, and he told me I must bring myself together. He said what was done was done, and I must forget it. Then I went into the rest room until I could be calmer.''

''So Victor was back there, too,'' I said, feeling better.

''Traci,'' Adam said, ''I don't think you can keep any of it a secret for very long. Other people know about it, and sooner or later someone will tell the police, if only to get themselves off the griddle.''

She sighed. ''I think you are right, Adam. I must hope they will believe me about the paintings. But mostly I must hope they will believe I did not kill Mark.''

"I think you should talk to a lawyer first," Adam said. "It'd be a good thing to know the best way to tell all, wouldn't it?"

"Kara West," I said. "She's my daughter's best friend, and according to Annie she's a whiz. And she'll talk to me on Saturday."

I went to call Kara while Adam and Traci cleared the table and loaded the dishwasher. Whether out of sympathy or friendship, Kara agreed to set up a meeting. I turned the phone over to Traci and joined Adam in the kitchen.

"What do you think of Victor Ingle as a suspect?" I asked.

Adam shrugged. "He's as good as anyone, I guess. Where do you want the rest of the muffins stashed?"

"Take them home, Adam. If they're here, I'll eat them. You know, if he and Duchat were partners, they could have had an argument."

"From what I hear, everyone in town could have had an argument with Duchat," Adam said.

Traci came into the kitchen just as the phone rang again.

I sighed. "Well, I'm getting my money's worth out of that stupid thing today."

It was Ellen. "Hi. Just thought I'd give you a little plot-thickening. Are you ready?"

"Just what I need, a thicker plot. So?"

"I was on my way to the deli this morning," she said. "Went by the late Mark Duchat's apartment building. Cops were there."

"So far so good," I said.

"Other times I would have gone on by," she said, "not being as nosy as certain other people. However, under the circumstances, I felt justified in asking a few polite questions of the super, who was standing around looking annoyed."

"And did the super answer your questions, oh tedious one?"

"You bet your boots, sweetie. Told me when the police

came to look the premises over, they found that someone had beaten them to it.''

''Someone broke in?''

''Yes indeed. Someone who was obviously searching very earnestly for something. Turned the place inside out. Cops are very displeased, as is the super.''

Chapter Eight

Henry's Hideaway was quiet on Sunday afternoon, and had the advantage of being removed from our telephones. Adam, Ellen, and I huddled in our favorite booth and considered the events that had taken over our lives.

"It wasn't a robbery," Adam said. "Whoever ransacked the apartment left some nice jewelry, a fair amount of money, all the appliances. Went through any papers they could find, emptied drawers, cupboards, bookcases."

"So they were just looking for something, something that would be written, letters, bills, or—um . . ." I stopped and chewed at a fingernail.

"Or," Adam added, "records. Records that could maybe incriminate someone."

I scowled at him. "Traci was at my place, not rooting through Mark Duchat's apartment."

"How do you know? We don't know when the place was searched."

"Adam," I said, "Traci did not kill Mark Duchat."

"I didn't say she did," he reminded me. "All I'm saying is that she had a reason to want to find whatever records he had on sales of her work."

"Now, now, kids," Ellen said. "Let's stop bickering. There were probably lots of people who wanted to find his paperwork."

"Who?" I asked, a bit snappishly. "The police seem fixated on Traci, as does Adam. Whom do you have in mind?"

"I don't know," she said. "But it seems to me that if

41

he was pulling a shady deal on Traci, he probably had other victims, too.''

Belva brought our sandwiches to the booth and we munched in gloomy silence.

''Well, okay,'' I said, swallowing the last of my dill pickle. ''We need names. Who wanted Mark Duchat dead?''

''Everyone who knew him,'' Ellen answered.

I bared my teeth at her. ''No flippancy here, if you don't mind. We'll get nowhere with hyperbole. No, everyone who knew the man apparently disliked him. That is not the same as wanting him dead. Many people probably just wanted him slapped around a little. What we want is someone who really wanted to kill him.''

''Not necessarily,'' Adam said, with his usual maddening desire for total accuracy. ''Considering that he was whacked with a weapon that was handy, it may have been spur-of-the-moment. In other words, not someone who flat out wanted him dead, but just went bananas all of a sudden.''

I sighed heavily. ''All right. Anyhow, under the circumstances, at least we can assume he was killed by someone who was at the gallery, right? I mean, he was there, very much alive, and then he was dead. So the killer was at the gallery, and had access to the office.'' This was progress!

Adam grinned. ''Don't work yourself into a corner,'' he warned. ''Most of the people there were your people. The girls, their families, the teachers, and whoever works at the gallery.''

''Plus a few friends, such as yourself,'' I said, narrowing my eyes at him. ''Okay, okay. We're pretty sure none of the nuns whacked him, and as far as I know none of the girls knew him from a cake of soap. We didn't do it. And Traci didn't.'' I glared at them, daring them to argue the point.

Ellen laughed. ''Okay, then, it's all settled. No one could have done the deed. Case closed.''

''You haven't mentioned Donald Tomcyk,'' Adam said.

''Oh, get serious!'' I said. ''Donald is . . . Donald is . . .''

"Donald is a friend of yours." Adam nodded. "So he couldn't be the bad guy, right?"

I gritted my teeth. "What about Sharon Cromwell?"

"I don't think that's likely," Adam said, "but she's a possibility."

"Why would she kill him?" Ellen asked.

"One thing at a time," I said. "Right now we're into opportunity. Motive comes later. What kind of detective are you?"

"Sorry. Okay, everyone there had the opportunity, so we're back where we started."

I sighed. "If you two are going to keep fighting me, I'm going to find new sidekicks. Now get with the program, will you? Besides being at the gallery, the murderer had to have access to the office. Sharon did, of course. Who else?"

"Everyone who was there," Ellen answered promptly. "Don't glare at me, Gen. It's true. The office is down the hallway, it wasn't locked, and anyone who went into the other showroom or to the rest rooms could have also gone to the office."

"Okay, how about this?" I asked. "Who else was with Duchat during the evening, someone who might have been mad enough to follow him back to the office to take care of unfinished business?"

"No one you want to hear about," Ellen said. "Traci. Donald. You and I. Sarah. Sharon. The only one you're willing to convict is Sharon, and I can't believe she'd kill someone in her own office during an exhibit."

"Duchat was in the side gallery for a while," Adam said, frowning in concentration. "He was talking to an older guy, gray hair, mustache."

"Were they arguing?" I asked hopefully.

"Couldn't tell you that. I was just coming from the rest room, not scouting for prospective killers."

"How unprescient of you, Adam," Ellen murmured.

I ignored her. "Well, when was that? Before or after he had his fracas with Donald?"

"After. A lot of people had left already."

"Well, there you are," I said, feeling much more cheerful. "A stranger, possibly the last person seen with the victim."

Ellen rolled her eyes. "Somewhat of a leap in logic, isn't it? This is your prime suspect, just because he's a stranger?"

"It's a start," I insisted. "Now, how many people could have been wandering around in the back rooms after Duchat was seen with this strange man? Sharon was in and out all evening, so she's still a suspect. I don't care what you think, Adam."

He grinned at me. "Okay, chief. Sharon and a strange man. That it?"

"I went back to the rest room toward the end," Ellen said. "There wasn't anyone in the side gallery then. I hope that doesn't put me on your short list."

"Not for now," I said. "Who else? Late in the evening, I mean."

"Sister Charlotte. Sarah. And . . ."

"And?"

"You won't like it," she warned. "Donald came out of the hallway just as I was headed there."

"And Traci," Adam reminded us.

I tried to ignore the mental picture of Traci, coming toward us, flushed and agitated. "I do not believe Traci . . ." I began.

"But what if she was there when someone else did it?" Adam said. "Someone she knew."

"Someone who was trying to protect her?" Ellen added.

There was a long moment of silence before I remembered that Donald had been standing with us when Traci came out.

"Why would they come out together?" Adam asked reasonably.

"All right, all right," I growled. "Put Donald on the

list! You're going to look very foolish when this case is solved, though.''

Ellen pulled out a notebook. ''So we have Sharon Cromwell, Donald Tomcyk, and . . .'' She wrote the names. ''. . . John Doe. That it?''

''What about that artist?'' I asked. ''Clint—Madison. He was really angry at Duchat.''

She looked doubtful. ''Was he at the gallery? I thought we were on opportunity . . .''

''Write him down anyway,'' I ordered, exasperated. ''We need more people on that list.''

''I don't think that's the way most people investigate crimes, Gen,'' she advised me. ''I mean, just picking out suspects because you need a longer list seems a little cavalier, don't you think?''

I narrowed my eyes at her, and she surrendered, writing *Clint Madison* on her list after *John Doe*.

''Now what?'' Adam asked, finishing his glass of beer. ''Do you have some kind of idea on what to do with this little list? I think the cops would expect something more than this to go on.''

''I know that,'' I said. ''As it happens, I do have some kind of idea. I think I will go and chat with Sharon Cromwell.''

Adam sat up sharply. ''You think you'll do what?''

''Are you nuts?'' Ellen said. ''Supposing she is the murderer, how do you imagine she'll take to your coming waltzing in and—''

''Oh, please!'' I said. ''What do you take me for? I'm not going to go in and ask her if she murdered Mark Duchat, for heaven's sake! I'm going to ask her who else may have been there, and who John Doe might be, and who else may have wanted the world rid of Duchat.''

''If she did it, she'll probably be only too happy to point to someone else,'' Ellen said.

''So at the least we'll have some more names for the list,'' I said confidently. ''It can't hurt.''

Chapter Nine

It was as if the whole school had been sucked into an electrical field. The moment I arrived on Monday morning I felt the crackling in the air.

Mr. Merryman, St. Phil's custodian, scowled from under his shaggy white eyebrows as we passed him that morning, as if trying to determine which of us should get the chair. Not that he ever views us with unqualified delight, but that Monday no doubt satisfied him that his original appraisal of us had proved correct.

The faculty lounge looked like the waiting room of a dentist who eschewed modern, painless techniques. Sarah dropped the tea tray. Donald slumped in the corner, owl-eyed.

Traci tore a paper napkin into ever-smaller pieces and nearly levitated when I spoke to her.

"Oh! Good morning, Geneviève. I am daydreaming." She made an effort to smile. "I am to see the lawyer this afternoon after lunch. I hope she will be able to help."

We all agreed that the lawyer would, indeed, have all the answers. So positive were we that Traci seemed to think we knew what we were talking about. She drew a deep breath and stopped making confetti.

"I have a package belonging to—to Mark at my apartment," she said. "He forgot it when he was there talking about—about the . . ." She glanced at me. "He was angry, you know. Anyhow, I want this to be returned to his apartment. I hope this lawyer will tell me how to do this. In

46

case the police come and search. I do not want things of his there."

"Of course," I said. "I'm sure Kara will know what to do."

The bell rang and we went forth into the shambles that once was a placid grove of academe, more or less. Even Sister Madonna was distracted, twice losing her train of thought during morning announcements, which was unheard of.

The seniors were drawn willy-nilly into the affairs of their usually ignorable teachers. The first period English Lit class fairly vibrated and I suspected Thackeray was going to get short shrift as long as a real-life melodrama was playing at the neighborhood school.

"Is it true that Miss Beaupré was arrested?" Lucy Bennett's brown eyes were wide as if in shock. She was one of Traci's art students.

"No," I said. "She was questioned, as we all were. Just so the police would have whatever facts might help them to solve the case."

"But the papers say she's going to be questioned again," Lucy said.

"Mrs. Galway, is it true that man was killed right when we were all there?" Candy Mankiewicz seemed torn between a desire for vicarious terror and an instinct for righteous anger.

I sighed. "The police assume so, yes. Now . . ."

"So . . ." Thelma Dudash said solemnly, "the killer was right there with us!"

A shudder rippled through the room.

"Actually," Rita Carstairs said, with a sly smile, "the killer might be one of us!"

A kill-the-messenger chorus erupted. "Well, it's true, isn't it?" Rita said, raising her voice above the rabble. "If he was killed at the gallery, it had to be by someone who was there, didn't it?"

"Nonsense!" I said. "Just settle down now. We are not auditioning for the 'Donahue' show. We are, instead, striving for admission into the college of our choice."

Reluctantly they allowed themselves to be diverted from the vicissitudes of real life to those of Victorian England, and I practiced pretending that I did not feel the current of dismay/fear/excitement/gloom pervading St. Philomena's.

At lunchtime I bought a salad in the cafeteria and retreated to the faculty lounge, where my fellow fugitives lurked. I had hoped for a respite from the murder du jour, but no such luck.

Bernadette Melendez, who taught gym and office skills, was relaying some information about Mark Duchat that she had gleaned from her husband. "Joe said he was hard to get to know. Very charming when he wanted to be, but wouldn't hesitate to stick a knife in your back if it served his purpose." Joe Melendez was the sports editor on the Derry *Sentinel*.

"Sounds like a familiar description," Ellen said. "Why does the *Sentinel* keep him if he's so unlovable?"

Bernadette shook her head and laughed, her dark curls bouncing. "Hey, controversy sells papers! And Mark Duchat was certainly controversial. The paper is always getting letters from artists who are furious at the guy. Of course, that just makes him try harder!"

"Doesn't he like *any* artists?" I asked. "Is he maybe in the wrong line of work?"

"I don't know. He's supposed to be an expert." She shrugged. "I'm not, so I have no idea whether the people he criticizes are any good. But it doesn't seem to me that they could all be that bad. Although that Starlight person, the one he wrote about a couple of weeks ago . . . ?"

"Ah, yes," Ellen said. "Omega Starlight."

"Yes." Bernadette nodded. "Well, we saw one of her performances, and she's real odd, believe me! She came right in to the office after Duchat's review, Joe said. She was really steamed. Joe said he could hear her yelling clear over in sports.''

''Really?'' I perked up. ''Did she maybe want to do him bodily harm?''

Bernadette grinned. ''Joe said she yelled something about cutting out his heart. How's that?''

''Nifty,'' I said, smiling meaningfully at Ellen. She scowled, but pulled out her notebook and added another name to the suspect list.

''Are you coming with us to see Sharon Cromwell after school?'' I asked Ellen.

''Can't,'' she said, not sounding too broken up about it. ''I have a yearbook committee meeting. But if you and Adam meet with foul play, I will let the police know who should be their prime suspect, never fear.''

I thanked her and went on to face the remnants of the day, smiling at the idea that I would fear Sharon Cromwell—I, who regularly faced a roomful of sophomore Phillies who were bent on destroying my sanity.

The electricity concentrated in soph English was enough to fuel at least a small city. I could almost see the girls' hair stand on end.

''Mrs. Galway, is it true that Miss Beaupré killed that man?'' Bridget Maguire attacked as soon as I entered.

''Certainly not!'' I said sternly. ''Who told you such a thing?''

''Well, but the television said she was being questioned, and—''

''And,'' Jean Ann interrupted, ''Miss Beaupré isn't here this afternoon, so . . .''

I glared at her. ''And is it your contention that whenever one of your teachers is absent, it indicates that she is a murderer?''

''Well, no, but . . .''

''But, Mrs. Galway,'' Denny Weisman said, ''he was Miss Beaupré's boyfriend, wasn't he? And . . .''

"And she was there, at the gallery," Bridget finished.

"And so was I," I reminded her. "And so was Sister Madonna. And many other people. How is it that such young and inexperienced folk as yourselves have managed to solve this crime before the police have done so?"

"Well, he *was* her boyfriend," Denny insisted.

"Many people do not kill their boyfriends," I told her.

"Mrs. Galway, did you see the—the—you know . . ."

"The body," Bridget said, bright eyes expectantly boring into me.

I sighed. "No. No, my dears, I did not see the body. I am sorry, but I did not know there would be a quiz. Now . . ."

Jean Ann wrinkled her pretty forehead. "No one did," she said, sounding aggrieved at the lack of curiosity shown by her supposed mentors.

"Except whoever killed him," Bridget chirped.

"Mrs. Galway," Christy said, "no one will tell us anything. I mean, the nuns just say tend to our own knitting, and Mr. Garfield wasn't there, and we can't ask Mr. Tomcyk, because—because—you know . . ."

"And Mrs. Galway, it isn't fair for no one to tell us, you know," Denny said. "Because it affects the school, after all."

"Yes," Bridget said. "And we could all be in danger, you know? I mean, if someone here is a murderer . . ."

I laughed in spite of myself. "Considering how often you tempt us, it doesn't seem likely, though, does it? None of your teachers has been driven to murder yet, no matter the provocation. Perhaps you'll just have to trust us."

Twenty faces reflected varying degrees of doubt.

"Anyway," Christy said, "Miss Beaupré couldn't have done it. She's too little to hit someone over the head hard enough to kill him. She's even smaller than you, Mrs. Galway."

"I take it that I am also exonerated, then? Thank you."

"I saw this show on TV?" Denny said. "About people

who were smuggling stolen paintings into this place? And someone found out and was blackmailing the smuggler. So they killed him.''

''And?'' I asked.

''Well, maybe that Duchat guy was meeting someone to get blackmail money, you know?''

''And,'' Bridget said, ''instead of paying him, they killed him.''

The bell rang to remind us that class was supposed to begin, and we turned to the vicissitudes of ''The Haunted Boy.''

The girls looked pleased at their deductions, and relieved that they had removed suspicion from anyone associated with St. Phil's. After all, none of us would be involved with stolen paintings.

I was not quite so pleased. I had the feeling that the would-be Nancy Drews had come a little too close for comfort to a scenario that the police would find plausible.

Chapter Ten

Sharon Cromwell laced her fingers together and rested her chin on them. "Who was here on Friday night besides the group from St. Philomena's? Let's see—there was a customer from Hebron who came to pick up a painting she left to be framed. A man who brought in a print to be cleaned and repaired. I don't think I ought to give you their names—they would possibly not be pleased to be brought into this mess."

She looked around the gallery and shook her head. The police had only Monday afternoon allowed her to reopen, and she had a desk set up in the small showroom, a make-shift office while her own was still off-limits. We had found her trying to get paperwork done while two employees cleaned up the mess left by patrons and police.

"I would like to help Traci, of course," she said. "It's preposterous to think she murdered Mark. However, the two customers I speak of were here early in the evening."

I nodded. "Right. I guess we're interested in people who were around at the time—uh . . ."

"Yes. Well, let me think." She got up and walked to the window and back. Sharon Cromwell was an elegant figure, about forty, I guessed, a little above average in height, with platinum hair in a French twist such as I had always wanted to achieve.

"Victor Ingle was here," she said, her lips tightening just for a moment. "He's a dealer in art and antiquities. He was supposed to pick up a piece that Mark was keeping here for him. I'm not sure when he came or went."

That was a familiar name. Where had I heard it?

Sharon continued. "Then . . . two or three artists were here at some point, bringing in or taking out. Mary may recall someone, of course. She won't be in today—she works only in the mornings. But she would have been here all day Thursday and Friday because of the exhibit. I'll ask her tomorrow and let you know."

"The artists who were here—was Clint Madison one of them?" I asked.

She thought for a moment. "I think so, yes. Why did you think of him in particular . . . Oh, I see! You witnessed the little contretemps between Clint and Mark the other day."

"It seemed worth considering," I said.

"Believe me, it wasn't too unusual." She smiled sardonically. "Mark took satisfaction in driving artists crazy, I think. But, Mrs. Galway, artists don't commit murder because of bad reviews. They may scream and threaten, or sit in a corner and sulk, or just pretend it doesn't matter. But they don't kill."

"Victor Ingle," I said, remembering where I had heard the name, and not wanting to mention that Traci had told us about him. "Seems to me I heard that he was involved in some questionable dealings."

"Really?" Sharon looked at me with just the right amount of interest one would normally show at a bit of gossip, but I saw her hands clench just for a second or two.

"I got the impression that you weren't very fond of Mr. Ingle," I said.

Her eyes held mine for an instant, then she looked away and a little color rose in her cheeks. After a moment, she said, still looking at a point over my head, "I found that Victor did business a shade less than ethically. Our relationship was not cordial after that."

"Did you ever report him?" Adam asked.

"To whom?" she asked, finally looking directly at us.

"Victor has many friends. Some of them have authenticated the artworks he's sold."

"You mean it's like a racket?" Adam stared at her. "Art experts in on making up phony documents for paintings?"

"Not exactly," Sharon said slowly. "Most of the experts are acting in good faith. Sometimes it's very difficult to be sure a piece is genuine; sometimes it comes down to instinct, and some people have very good instincts. But it often depends on the rapport between the museum curators or professors and the dealer. Victor Ingle is a very charming man when he chooses to be. And I am not in a position to make enemies."

"But it is a lucrative business, dealing in forgeries?" I asked.

"It certainly can be. Often more so than stealing the real thing, and with less chance of being caught."

"And Mark Duchat," I said. "Was he in on it?"

She hesitated just a hair too long. "I'm sure I don't know. I never got involved in Victor's business."

"Ms. Cromwell," I said gently. "That day we brought the pieces over here for the show, the day we saw Duchat and Madison arguing—you seemed less than pleased to see Mark. You wanted to know what he was doing here. And he said something about Victor telling you he was coming." I waited.

She studied her hands for a long moment before raising her eyes and returning my gaze. "You are observant, aren't you? Well, you're right, I wasn't at all pleased to see Mark Duchat. I had found out that he was working with Victor, that he had provided some of the works Victor sold me. I was furious, of course. I told Victor I expected him to make it right, quietly, or I'd go to the authorities." She paused.

"And . . . ?" I prompted.

"He said he'd talk to Mark, that Mark had the records. The day you were here, that was what he had come to talk about."

"What was he going to do?" Adam asked.

"He agreed to provide the records of the forgeries, so that I could contact my buyers. He also agreed to take responsibility for the 'mistake' in authenticating the paintings."

"And no legal complications?" I said.

She smiled ironically. "Mrs. Galway, buyers of expensive art do not usually like to notify the world that they have been taken. Their reputation as connoisseurs is far more important to them than bringing art thieves to justice."

"So now that Duchat is dead, you may be out of luck as far as getting this straightened out," Adam said.

"I'm afraid so. Unless someone finds the records, I'll have a hard time finding out which pieces were forgeries. If we call in experts it'll mean notifying every buyer and starting a real imbroglio."

I stood up. "Well, thanks for taking the time to talk to us, Ms. Cromwell. If you think of anything else that might help, would you call me?"

She wrote my name and number on her phone pad, and promised to keep us in mind.

"So what do you think?" I asked Adam after we buckled ourselves into his T-Bird. "Is she still on our suspect list?"

"Dunno." He drummed his fingers on the wheel. "If she's telling the truth, she had more to lose than to gain by his death, right?"

"Well, I don't know if she loses, exactly," I said. "Depends on how badly she wanted to tell her buyers they were cheated. They might not be pleased with her either, you know. Also . . ." I was trying to sort out my impressions.

"Also?"

"You said 'if she's telling the truth.' I was just thinking about her saying that Mark agreed to take the blame for the false authentication. Somehow that doesn't sound like his style."

"Good point," Adam agreed. "And if she lied about

that, she may be lying about other things." He started the car and eased out into traffic.

"Besides Sharon," I said, "maybe we have another suspect. If Duchat was going to admit to the phony art deals, where did that leave Victor Ingle?"

"Or if Duchat was going to blame Ingle for the 'mistakes,' which sounds a lot more likely . . ."

"Yes!" I said. "That could have made him mad enough to hit Duchat over the head. It could also make him want to search Duchat's apartment for any records that would incriminate him."

Adam maneuvered around a double-parked delivery truck and swung into Beacon Street. "Certainly possible."

"So," I said, "why don't we go chat with Mr. Ingle?"

"Forget it," Adam said. "I agreed to go and see Cromwell because we did have at least a quasi-innocent reason to talk to her. It's her gallery, she knows Traci, etc. But Ingle is another story. You don't have any reason to drop in and chat with him, and unless he's real stupid, he'd know that."

"But . . ."

"Hey, Genny, we aren't detectives. Amateurs who go poking around trying to solve crimes are more likely to join the victims on the next slab. If Ingle is a killer, he might be perfectly willing to add you to his list." He made the turn into Locust Street.

"Well, I certainly wouldn't tell him I think he . . ."

"I'm not negotiating this," he said, frowning at me. "What I'm going to do is tell Frank Monroe about the scam. He's a good cop, Gen. Let him handle it."

"But the police already think they've got their man—woman," I argued. "Unless they have some proof . . ."

"No." Adam said it with an air of finality. He pulled over in front of my building, and I got out.

"It'll work out, Gen," he said. "But you're off the case now."

Well, that's what *he* thought.

Chapter Eleven

"Tell me again why you're doing this," I said, looking over Ellen's shoulder at the stack of high school yearbook photos she was flipping through, photos of the long-suffering faculty members of St. Phil's. Sarah, Bernadette, and Traci, sipping their morning coffee, crowded around the table to have a look.

"It's part of our religious formation," she said. "A little humiliation builds character."

In their never-ending quest to build the characters of their elders and betters, the *Beacon* staff was running a series featuring our high school photos and accompanying bios. Not all of us were pleased, but Sister Madonna had approved it. Victims to be spotlighted in the next issue were: Donald J. Tomcyk—Student council president. Varsity letters in football and track. Likes computers, pizza, and J.R.R. Tolkien. Two brothers, two sisters. Sister Ursula M. Kennedy—Glee Club. 4-H. Likes swimming, dancing, the Beatles. Four sisters. Sarah A. Joplin—Class secretary. Letter in basketball. Likes photography, camping. One brother. And Genevieve M. Lacy—Drama club. Tennis team. Likes bicycling, dancing, reading, and hot fudge sundaes. One sister, one brother.

I was sorry to see that none of the others looked as goofy as I.

"Are they going to run one on Mr. Merryman?" I asked.

"Mr. Merryman had no youth," Ellen said. "He arrived at St. Phil's with the cornerstone, designed specifically to terrorize errant teachers."

58   *Elizabeth Wetzel*

"Lucky devil," I said.

The first bell rang and we gathered our belongings.

"Now where has my purse gone?" Traci asked. "I am becoming so scatter-minded!"

"Maybe you left it in your classroom," Sarah said, after a quick search failed to turn it up.

Traci sighed. "Maybe. I hope I will soon think normally again."

Her meeting with Kara West the day before had helped. Although she still looked tired and pale, she was less jittery, and she had plans, she said, to go out for dinner that evening, a prospect that brought a small smile to her face.

In fact, all of us were much improved Tuesday. The Phillies turned their attention back to their own business, which involved who had dates for the Central High dance, who was going to try out for the spring play, whether Peggy Rinaldi's father was really going to buy her a car for graduation, and when we were going to hear the results of the Chesterton Scholarship exam. In between these pressing concerns, they did some class work.

After lunch, Traci's purse turned up in the auditorium, and was returned by Mr. Merryman, along with a lecture about leaving things around where them young devils could get hold of them, never knowing what they'd do, and us teachers had got to start being more careful; we couldn't expect him to always be finding our things.

Even the American Lit class was back to normal, not that that was something to brag about. By Tuesday, Bridget and Christy had decided to pin the crime on Omega Starlight, on the grounds that she was obviously using a phony name.

"You know, Mrs. Galway," Bridget said, "if she didn't have something to hide, she wouldn't use an alias. That's what criminals do, right?"

"That's not an alias," Denny objected. "It's a—like a pen name, like Mark Twain or—um—O. Henry. A pseudonym, that's what."

We have these occasional epiphanies wherein I learn that they have been paying attention at odd moments. "Very good," I said. "Yes, artists and writers sometimes use pseudonyms in their professional lives. It doesn't mean they're involved in criminal activities."

"Anyhow," Denny said, "a criminal would pick a name that sounded ordinary, not something that everyone would notice."

Bridget and Christy looked disappointed.

"Maybe it's a nickname," Jean Ann said. "So she couldn't help it." Everyone stared at her, including me, although we all know by now that Jean Ann often drifts off into a land untraveled by the rest of us.

Denny sighed. "What does that have to do with anything, Jean Ann? And why would anyone have a nickname like 'Omega'?"

"Well, I don't know. People just get nicknames. Because their real names are too kind of serious. Everyone gets nicknames."

"I don't," Bridget said.

I glanced at the clock, longing for the bell that would demand the beginning of class. These discussions sometimes take a lot out of me.

"Well, most people do," Jean Ann insisted. "Like Denny, for Denise. Or Miss Beaupré being Traci, for Thérèse. Do you have a nickname, Mrs. Galway?"

"Yes," I said, just as the bell finally rang. "It's Ma'am. Now, let's spend a little time with Theodore Dreiser. His nickname was Ted, but you may call him that only after you feel you really know him."

Yes, a normal day, a day to give confidence that things could be sorted out with a little common sense. Which is what I planned for my after-school activities.

Chapter Twelve

It was still cold, but the sun was shining, which I took as a good omen.

"Do we really know what we're doing?" Ellen asked as we turned into Faraday Street, in the high-rent district.

"Certainly," I said. "We're going to find out how Victor Ingle felt about his partner in crime."

"Yes. So you explained when you talked me into this trip. However, as we approach the moment of truth, I am having second thoughts. What if he's annoyed at our questions?"

I laughed. "Oh, don't be such a worrywart. As I tried to explain to Adam, I'm not planning to accuse him of murder. I told you what I'm going to say."

"Hmmm." She looked gloomy. "Okay. But if he pulls out a gun and shoots us, I'm going to be really irritated at you."

I pulled into the parking lot beside the Towson Building, an imposing gray edifice adorned with carved gargoyles, where V. I. Enterprises was located. My Escort looked small and meek among the Mercedeses, Porsches, and BMWs, but I ensconced it firmly between a red MG and a yellow Porsche, and urged Ellen out. "You watch too much television," I said. "Come on. Excelsior!"

V. I. Enterprises was on the third floor, just opposite the elevator. I opened the heavy door and stepped into a reception area carpeted in forest-green plush soft enough to sleep on, and approached the carefully sculpted receptionist who presided over the mahogany desk.

"How may I help you?" Her voice was low and melodious, her smile perfectly designed.

"We would like to speak to Mr. Ingle," I said, trying for a low, melodious tone in return, and noting that she did not seem impressed.

"Have you an appointment?"

"I'm afraid not," I said, this time trying to sound regretful yet assertive. "It is, however, very important that we see him. We won't need much of his time." Even to myself it sounded more obsequious than assertive, and it was clear that Ms. Receptionist wasn't fooled at all.

"Mr. Ingle's schedule is very heavy today," she said, demonstrating how to sound regretful yet assertive. "If you would care to leave a message for Mr. Ingle, or to make an appointment for another time . . . ?"

I thought fast. "We need to talk to Mr. Ingle about Mark Duchat," I said. "About some information we've received."

There was the slightest flicker of some emotion on the flawless face, and I hoped I had hit a button. "If it's just a rumor, we don't want to bother the police, but . . ."

Beside me, Ellen sucked in her breath. I ignored her. Ms. Receptionist smiled again, but a bit stiffly.

"If you'll wait for a moment, I'll just see if Mr. Ingle has a few minutes before his next appointment." She looked at us with obvious distaste and glided through the imposing door behind her desk.

"Why did you say that?" Ellen whispered, poking me. "Have you lost your mind? You said you weren't going to tell the man we've got him on our suspect list. I swear . . ."

I shushed her as the door to Ingle's office opened and the receptionist reappeared.

"Mr. Ingle can give you just a few minutes," she purred, looking as if she would prefer to snarl, but was too well bred.

Victor Ingle's office was dressed to impress, with forest-green satin draping the window, a clutch of three chairs clad in gray with narrow cherry-red stripes, a bronze abstract sculpture beside the door, and just the right number of paintings spaced on the silvery gray walls. The man himself stood behind a softly gleaming antique desk that held a Tiffany lamp and a small pewter figurine. If Adam's descriptive powers had been adequate, I'd bet he was our John Doe: maybe an inch short of six feet tall, somewhat rotund, wearing a smoothly welcoming expression. His iron-gray hair matched his mustache, and both were in meticulous array, as was his blue silk suit.

He smiled as we waded through another expanse of plush, and gestured to two Sheraton chairs in front of his desk. "Please, have a seat. I'm sorry I have so little time today, but I am, of course, interested in any information about this tragedy. Naturally, I want to help in any way I can to find Mr. Duchat's murderer. I understood that the police had a suspect in mind."

We obediently sat, and Ingle settled into the chair behind his desk and gazed at us with eyes you could sharpen steel with.

"Mr. Ingle," I said, arranging my face in what I hoped was a guileless look, "we are just sure that Traci Beaupré was not responsible. She is a colleague of ours, you know, and, my goodness, we just can't imagine that she would do such a thing!"

He nodded understandingly. "Well, I'm sure it's hard for all of us to believe someone we know could be a murderer. Your loyalty does you credit. But I'm afraid I don't see how I can help you. You had information, you said?"

"Oh, yes. Well, rumors, really. Ordinarily I wouldn't want to even pay attention. But to help Traci, well, my goodness, we have to pay attention to everything, don't we? I mean, you just don't know what may be important."

"Oh, indeed. And what are these rumors, Mrs. Galway?"

I was pleased to see that the flinty eyes had softened, and Ingle was looking at me with the condescending look reserved for cute children and not-quite-bright women. I'd have to remember this persona for the next appropriate role in the community theater.

"Well, it has something to do with forgeries," I said. "Forged paintings, I believe. Mr. Duchat is supposed to have been selling them. And—um . . ." I hesitated fetchingly.

"Yes?" Ingle picked up a pencil and examined it carefully.

"And," I said timidly, "there is talk that he had a partner. Well, that you were his partner, Mr. Ingle. Now, you can see why we wouldn't want to just go and tell the police that, because, you know, it could cause trouble for someone who might be quite innocent. So we all talked it over and thought we ought to speak to you about it first."

"All of you?" Ingle's eyes were still on his slowly twirling pencil. "Who might that include?"

"Why, all of us at the school. We all believe Traci is innocent, you see." It certainly was true that we all believed Traci was innocent, and if we had all known about the forgeries, we would have talked it over. Besides, I thought it was less likely that Ingle, supposing he was the killer, would risk killing a whole faculty, including nuns, than just Ellen and me.

He raised his eyes and looked at me speculatively. "And where did you hear this story, Mrs. Galway?"

"From Traci Beaupré," I said, meeting his eyes. "She found that her paintings were being sold as works by master artists. She was very upset."

He took time out to smooth his mustache before responding mildly, "If true, that would seem to provide a motive for your friend. She and Duchat were, I understand, romantically involved. Learning that he had taken advantage of their relationship must have made her very angry."

"Yes," I agreed. "But, of course, we are quite sure Traci is innocent. And if she is innocent, then someone else might be considered a suspect. If the story is true, that is."

"Mrs. Galway." He put down the pencil and leaned across the desk. "If, as you suspect, I was Duchat's partner, why would I want to kill him? I assume that is your point?"

I sighed. "This is most difficult, Mr. Ingle. I do hope you understand that we don't want to be rude, but, yes, I'm afraid that thought had occurred to us. You see, we had also heard that Mr. Duchat was found out. That would affect the partnership, wouldn't it? And possibly the partner as well."

"And where did you hear that bit of news?" Ingle's voice had lost its tone of wry amusement.

I hesitated for only a second. "From Sharon Cromwell. According to her, Mr. Duchat agreed to admit to mistakes in authenticating the paintings she had sold."

Ingle laughed, a short, sharp bark. "She told you that? Tell me, Mrs. Galway, how well did you know Mark Duchat?"

"Not well. Only through Traci."

"Ah. If you knew him at all well, you would realize the unlikelihood of Mark Duchat's ever 'admitting' to anything."

And Adam and I had figured that much, of course.

"Duchat was a con man," he continued. "He liked to play games. I think it was the challenge of cheating people that he liked, even more than the money he acquired. If Sharon says he was going to help her make things right, she's lying."

"Well," I said slowly, "maybe he intended to put the blame on someone else. Maybe his partner."

A muscle twitched in Ingle's cheek. "That sounds more like him, yes. But if I were his—partner—I would never have killed him; I'd have to have been insane. You see, Duchat was a record keeper. It was a big thing for him. He liked to let people know that he had everything on the record. And no one knew where he kept his records. Including me." He smiled coldly. "Duchat's death was not good news for anyone who did business with him, Mrs. Galway, I assure you.''

''Someone searched Duchat's apartment,'' Ellen said, and I jumped, having forgotten she was there.

Ingle glared at her. ''Well, it wasn't I. I wouldn't waste my time. As I told you, Mark was a game player. I'd never expect to find important records in his apartment, at least not in any recognizable form.''

He stood, a signal that our interview was over, and we obediently moved toward the door.

Ingle stopped us at the threshold. ''You might want to put Sharon Cromwell on your list of people who had been stung by Duchat. In more ways than one.''

''Meaning?'' I asked.

''Meaning, my dear Mrs. Galway, that Sharon Cromwell and Mark Duchat go back a lot farther than you might have suspected.'' He smiled an icy smile that matched his eyes, and closed the door on us.

We mushed across the reception area, feeling the receptionist's eyes on our backs, and escaped.

''Well, that was some performance,'' Ellen snapped. ''Who were you being, Miss Marple's half-witted sister?''

''It worked, didn't it?''

''Worked? What worked? You accused the man of murder, and convinced him that you're non compos mentis at the same time.''

''He told us some things we didn't know,'' I reminded her. ''Excelsior!''

Chapter Thirteen

The old warehouse district had been converted to lofts and studios several years ago. Clint Madison's studio was above an interior decorator's place, reached by an outdoor staircase.

Ellen wasn't being a good sport about our visit at all, though I had pointed out that the studio was right on our way home from V. I. Enterprises, and that therefore it would be silly to pass up the opportunity to check Clint out.

"I never thought you'd be such a scaredy-cat," I said. "Where's your spirit of adventure?"

"I don't have a spirit of adventure," she snapped. "All my life I've tried to avoid the adventures you've dragged me into."

I sighed. "Are you going to bring up the broken arm again? That was over forty years ago, for heaven's sake."

"As a matter of fact, no. I was going to bring up the roller-skating incident. Or the jumping-from-the-garage-roof-to-the-tree incident. Or . . ."

"Okay, okay. This is different."

"My mother said you were a terrible kid. And you were. Are."

We had reached the top of the steps. I flapped my hand at Ellen and opened the door into a bare hallway with a door on either side. The one to our left bore a sign announcing *PERSONAL EFFECTS, Creations by K. B. Zandorph.* From behind the unadorned door to our right came a sound like a large animal being beaten vigorously with guitars. After knocking several times, with a predictable lack of response, I decided, over Ellen's vehement protests, to open the door a crack and peek in.

Clint Madison stood with his back toward us, facing a panel about the size of a billboard. In one fist he held a large brush which he was wielding like a weapon against the painting, a phantasmagoria of violently clashing colors. Canvases of various sizes stood against two walls, leaned against a table holding an assortment of dishes and glasses, rested on a lumpy sofa. A stereo system dominated the third wall and emitted the sounds of mayhem we had noted from outside.

"Excuse me?" I couldn't even hear myself, and it was painfully obvious that my well-bred little overture wasn't going to make it across the room. I didn't know what the protocol was for entering an artist's studio; was it a semi-public place, like an office? Or more like a home, which one had to be invited to enter? Reasoning that if one wasn't supposed to enter uninvited, one would have found the door locked, I opted for sophistry, pushed the door open farther, and ventured across the sill.

Taking a deep breath, I shouted, *"Excuse me?"* just as the recording died a merciful death and my voice exploded into the ensuing silence, shocking me so that I stepped backward and bumped into Ellen.

Madison's head swiveled in our direction, then back to his work. "Yeah?"

I gulped. "I'm sorry! I didn't intend to shout at you, Mr. Madison. The music . . ."

"Yeah," he said. "Wake the dead."

"I beg your pardon?"

He jerked his head toward the stereo. " 'Wake the Dead.' You know them?"

"Ah." I shook my head. "Um—no, I can't say I do."

"Great sound," he said. "They'll be on top one day, if they can get past the clods who run the industry."

"Really?"

He put down his brush and picked up a spatula. "It's all politics, of course. Like everything else. Everything's rotten politics." He made a sudden lunge and flung a glob of electric-blue paint at the panel. Ellen yanked at my sleeve.

"Do I know you?" Madison turned to face us, wiping his hands on a multicolored rag.

"N-no," I said. "I don't think so. We saw you at the Cromwell Gallery." I introduced us, to his obvious lack of interest.

"You looking for a painting?" he asked, eying us doubtfully. "A sculpture?"

"Actually no," I said. "Not today, that is. We just, um, wanted to talk to you. If you have a minute, that is."

He shrugged, walked to a table, pawed around among various pieces of junk. "Shoot." He picked up a length of chain and weighed it appraisingly.

I tried to remember why I had thought this would be a good idea. Clint Madison looked bigger than I recalled. "Well, the thing is . . ." My voice sounded as if it were being piped in from some far outpost. I cleared my throat. "Well, I suppose you've heard about the—the incident at the gallery. The m-murder, that is. At the gallery."

Madison looked over his shoulder at me. "Yeah. So?"

I took a deep breath that didn't seem to reach my lungs. "Yes. So, the police seem to think a friend of ours might be involved. And we thought . . ."

Ellen yanked my sleeve again.

"We thought if we knew more about Mark Duchat, maybe we could think of someone else who—who . . ."

Madison glowered at me, and I rattled ahead, words tumbling faster and faster, like an old windup Victrola wound too tight. "And since he is—was—an art critic, we thought you might have know him, since you are an art—artist, and maybe you could tell us what he w-was like . . ."

"What he was like?" Madison took two giant steps toward us, the chain swinging from his upraised fist, his face a deep mottled red.

"Ipp!" Ellen squeaked. I would have squeaked, too, if my heart had not suddenly stopped beating and left me speechless.

"You want to know what Duchat was like?" Shake, shake, rattle, rattle. "He was a pimple on the face of the earth, that's what he was like! He was a social disease! Art critic! He wouldn't have known a work of art if it came up and bit him on the nose!"

I was by that time backed firmly against Ellen, who was backed firmly against the door, which we had foolishly closed behind us. I stood there, pelted with exclamation marks, eying the gyrations of the chain, trying to say the act of contrition, which seemed to have fled my mind in this my hour of apparent need.

"The only thing Duchat had to do with art was to try to tear everyone down," Madison said, ponytail flying as he whipped around and stomped toward his painting-in-progress, which he proceeded to flail with the chain.

" ' . . . to confess my sins, to do penance and to amend my life, amen,' " I muttered, teeth chattering.

My first choice, to flee the premises, seemed closed, since I was unable to move my feet. However, feeling was returning to my mouth.

"Well," I said faintly, "it did seem as if he came down pretty hard on local artists. It didn't seem at all fair." I thought it might be a good idea to let him know we were on his side.

"Fair? You want to see fair?" He flung down the chain and stalked over to a canvas-covered object in the corner. Yanking the canvas aside, he beckoned us. "Look here!"

It sounded like a command, and before I had a chance to weigh my response, my unwilling feet had carried me across the room. A clay object, about three feet tall, stood on a small table. It resembled a free-form bird that had been struck by lightning while in flight. Madison stared at me expectantly.

"Hmmm," I said, nodding sagely. "Yes."

"That's a model of the sculpture for the atrium at the city building. The sculpture that was *supposed* to be in the atrium, that is." He gave me a fierce frown.

Brain cells clicked and revolved. Just as I was about to give up, a small voice traveled from the doorway, where craven Ellen had stayed.

"It was m-mentioned in the r-review," she quavered.

"Yes!" Madison bellowed. "I won that contract fair and square! It was just about to be signed. Then after that dirt-bag wrote his column, the spineless creeps at city hall backed out. Fair!"

"Oh, my," I said. "How awful for you." Well, so I don't come up with memorable dialogue under pressure.

"You know why he did that?"

I shook my head.

"Two years ago I got an award from the Midwest Arts Consortium," Madison said. "An award that Duchat wanted to go to one of his toadies. He was out to get me ever since. That's what Duchat was like."

"I can see why you'd dislike him," I said. It was time to quit, I assured myself. Quit while we were still alive. *We are not detectives,* I reminded myself, and this man was angry enough to be dangerous. So it was time to say good-bye and leave.

Unfortunately, I seldom listen to good advice, even from myself, and I was horrified, but not surprised, to hear myself continue. "You were there, weren't you, Mr. Madison? At the g-gallery? The night of the m-murder?"

Behind me I heard a gasp, and heard the door open stealthily.

Madison, staring at his model, answered in a distracted voice. "Yeah, I think so. I was . . ." He stopped suddenly, his head jerking toward me, and unbelievably, he laughed. Thank goodness.

"You want to know if I killed him? Listen, I'm shedding no tears for the guy. As far as I'm concerned, whoever offed him did a service for humanity. But it wasn't me. I didn't even see the creep that night.''

He flipped the canvas over the model again and ambled toward his painting. ''The cops think it was a friend of yours, huh? Well, sorry I can't help you out. Unless you can get me on her jury.'' He laughed again, and I joined in feebly. ''Tell you what, though,'' he said, picking through his brushes. ''Don't give up. Heck, there must be dozens of people who would have been happy to bash Duchat. Keep looking.''

I moved toward the door. ''Well, thanks. Uh, any ideas about who some of those people might be?''

He shrugged. ''Cromwell, maybe. They had some history. Some of the other artists he trashed.''

I remembered his fellow target in Duchat's column. ''Omega Starlight?'' I asked.

''Why not? She's as weird as anyone else.'' He started dabbing at the painting, and I took it we were dismissed.

Ellen was already in the hall, steeped in outrage. She gave me one bilious look and turned, stomping down the stairs and out to the car.

''Well, that was interesting,'' I said, trying for a casual tone, eying Ellen cautiously.

She seethed in silence while I started the car and moved out.

''You are insane,'' she said finally. ''Do not, I repeat, do not ever even try to get me into one of these situations again.''

''Oh, Ellen . . .''

She ignored me. ''Actually, *I* am insane. Why else would I let you do these things to me? Well, never again.''

''Oh, come on, Ellen . . .''

''And,'' she said, ''I'm going to tell Adam what you've been up to. I hope it's against the law, and they'll put you away. You are a menace.''

And she refused to say another word all the way home.

Chapter Fourteen

"I can't believe you did such a harebrained thing," Adam said, scowling at me. "You're an intelligent woman, for Pete's sake. Tell me what the heck you were thinking."

True to her word, Ellen had tattled to Adam the first chance she got. She sat across the booth from us, looking abused and munching on a Belva Burger, which was turkey trying to be tasty.

I sighed. "Well, but Adam, we did find out . . ."

"You could have been killed," he said. "You still might be, if you got the killer thinking you know too much. Did you think of that?"

"Well, but Adam, we . . ."

"She won't admit she did anything stupid," Ellen said. "She never does. Let me tell you, she was scared witless in Clint Madison's studio, but will she admit it now? Nooo!"

"I will admit it! Okay? Nevertheless, we did find out some things, and since we already risked our lives, you might as well listen."

Adam scowled at me again for good measure and picked up his corned beef sandwich. "I'm listening."

"Okay. We found out that Sharon Cromwell knew Duchat better than she let on—Victor Ingle and Clint both mentioned that. So, if she lied about that, maybe she had a reason to kill him."

He nodded grudgingly.

"Also, Duchat was a record-keeper, but liked to play games, so no one knew where he kept them."

"So?"

"So maybe there are things in his records that would help us figure out who killed him."

"The records that no one can find," Ellen said.

"One thing at a time. Anyhow, that was probably why someone broke into Duchat's apartment. And Ingle could still be guilty, even though the missing records are bad news for him. If the murder wasn't planned, if he just got mad and did it without thinking about the consequences . . ."

Adam swallowed. "Yeah. And now he knows you suspect him. So maybe his next murder will be planned."

"Oh, Adam! Anyhow, then there's Clint Madison. He was mad enough to kill, and he had a pretty good reason. And he was at the gallery the night of the murder."

"In his favor, you might consider that he didn't bash your heads in while he had you handy," Adam said.

I ignored that. "And there's Omega Starlight, although I admit that's just a passing thought."

"Well, that's all very interesting," Adam said. "But it doesn't seem like the kind of evidence worth risking your life for."

"Exactly," Ellen said.

"I didn't risk my life," I said. Ellen rolled her eyes. "Anyhow, I think it's worth talking to Sharon again, just to see . . ."

"What did I just say?" Adam asked. "Are you nuts? No more investigating. I will pass on your information to Marino and Monroe. Although they probably know all about it, you realize. They aren't stupid."

"But they think Traci is guilty," I argued. "So maybe they aren't as interested in finding out about all these other people. For instance, I'll bet they don't know about Clint Madison."

Adam sighed. "So I'll tell them."

"And Omega Starlight," I said. "There wouldn't be

anything wrong with paying her a visit, just to see what she's like.''

"See?'' Ellen said. "She's going to do it, Adam. I'm telling you. I know that look.''

He blew out an exasperated breath and examined the ceiling for a time while I finished my tuna sandwich. Ellen watched me, drumming on the table.

Finally Adam turned an evil eye in my direction. "All right. We'll stop over at the station and give the real detectives your information. Then they'll tell you to stay out of it. Then I'll take you home.''

I smiled at him. Ellen snorted.

"If the cops say, 'Oh, very good, keep on with your investigating, we love to get help from amateur busybodies,' then I'll go along with you anywhere you want to poke around. Okay?'' Adam smiled back, but his smile was not what you would call friendly.

"Okay,'' I agreed.

Ellen declined to join us, insisting that she was through with the entire case. Adam and I headed downtown, but I prevailed upon him to stop at Traci's first, to ask if she had any more information about Clint Madison or Victor Ingle.

Traci's apartment occupied the second floor of an old house on a quiet street of similarly converted homes about ten blocks from my own place. As soon as we opened the outside door we could hear a babble of voices from upstairs. Before we reached the stairway, Mrs. Todd, the first-floor resident, rushed out of her apartment. She almost levitated when she saw us, then recovered, smacking herself in the chest as if attempting cardiac resuscitation.

"Oh, it's you, Mrs. Galway! You gave me such a scare!''

"I'm sorry, Mrs. Todd,'' I said, reaching out to pat her shoulder. "What's wrong?''

"Oh, it's such a shock, in this neighborhood, why, we've never had anything like this . . . and those poor little girls! They shouldn't be there alone . . .''

She scuttled for the stairs, with Adam and me at her heels.

"I just got home, just a few minutes ago," she panted. "Right after the girls got here, poor little things. I just can't believe it, right here in this neighborhood. And the Camdens next door being on vacation, maybe the police should check their house, too. You never know, do you?"

We reached the top of the stairs before I could get a word in edgewise, to find, hovering at Traci's open door, the poor little things who were the objects of Mrs. Todd's concern. They were Lucy Bennett and Rita Carstairs, two of the senior Phillies, and both of them looked like death.

"Oh, Mrs. Galway!" Rita stared at me. "How did you know about it?"

"Isn't it awful?" Lucy asked. "Poor Miss Beaupré!"

"What? What?" I grabbed Rita's arm. "What's happened to Miss Beaupré?"

"Not to her," Rita said. "To her apartment. Isn't that why you're here?"

I shook my head and released her. "What about her apartment?"

"Someone was there and pulled books and papers out," Lucy said.

"See, we came to see Miss Beaupré," Rita explained. "We just wanted to tell her we don't think she killed anyone. She wouldn't do that, you know."

"And when we got there," Lucy chimed in, "we knocked on the door, and it opened. And so we called to Miss Beaupré."

"But she didn't answer," Rita said. "So we looked in. And we could see a lamp had fallen off a table. So Lucy said maybe Miss Beaupré fell or fainted or something and we should look."

"And we went in," Rita said, shivering suddenly. "And there were books and papers all over, and drawers open and stuff. We were going to look in the bedroom and kitchen, to see if Miss Beaupré was hurt, but—but . . ."

Her eyes filled with tears and she looked at me beseech-ingly.

"W-we thought we heard a n-noise in the b-bedroom," Lucy said. "And we ran out."

"We were r-really scared, Mrs. G-Galway!" Rita's chin quivered.

I put my arm around her. "Of course you were scared. Who wouldn't have been?"

Lucy cleared her throat and said more steadily, "So we ran downstairs to get help, and the woman there said she'd call the police. I guess the burglar got away." She looked mournful.

"I called the police," Mrs. Todd said, nodding vigor-ously. "Now, don't you worry about it."

I ventured into the apartment. *Not a burglar,* I thought. The things that burglars carried off were still there: the VCR, a tape recorder, a laptop computer, some very nice objets d'art.

No, not a burglar. Someone looking for something.

Lucy and Rita were recovering their composure and had inched their way into the room, leaving Mrs. Todd cow-ering in the hall and bending Adam's ear. Careful to touch nothing, the girls sidled over to me.

"Mr. Duchat gave Miss Beaupré that painting," Lucy said.

I followed her gesture and gazed at a small oil painting sitting on a chair by the desk.

"She had it on the wall," Lucy said, "but I guess she took it down after—after . . ."

"I don't think she liked it very much," Rita said. "Even though she said it was very well done. I think she only hung it up because it was a gift."

"It's Ste. Thérèse, you know," Lucy said. "Miss Beau-pré's namesake. Her real name is Thérèse."

I remembered that. "It's an odd painting of Ste. Thérèse, though, isn't it?" I said, trying to decide just what about it was wrong.

Rita nodded. "She's holding the wrong flowers. She usually holds roses."

This Thérèse was carrying tulips, and what looked like African violets, pretty strange for a bouquet. And there was something else . . . "She has a Mona Lisa face," I said. "Mr. Duchat was a most peculiar man."

Noises from downstairs announced the arrival of the police, and the girls went scurrying back to the door to greet them. I lingered in front of the painting, frowning at the inscription on the bottom: *Les fleurs du mal*. Ste. Thérèse is sometimes known as "The Little Flower." But the flowers referred to in the inscription had nothing to do with the good saint. *Les fleurs du mal*—the flowers of evil. A poem; rather, a collection of poems. By Baudelaire, I thought. And what in heaven's name did that have to do with Ste. Thérèse? A peculiar man indeed, Mark Duchat.

Sgt. Monroe came in, responding to a mere burglary because it involved his favorite suspect, no doubt. He surveyed the apartment—and me—while his minions talked to Lucy and Rita. After assuring themselves that the girls knew nothing else, they let them go and turned their attention to the apartment. Frank graciously allowed me to explain why we were not dealing with a burglar.

"Nothing missing—as far as you know—and no forced entry; either she left her door unlocked or someone had a key." Frank rubbed his nose. "Any idea where your friend might be?"

I shook my head. "She was going out to dinner, but I don't know when she was expected home. We just stopped in case she was back, because I wanted to ask her— um . . ." I stopped, wondering if now would be a good time to share the rest of my theories.

He gave me a suspicious look.

"Anyway," I said hurriedly, "this proves she isn't the murderer."

He smiled. "Not exactly."

"What? But surely she didn't search her own apartment!

Whoever killed Mark Duchat is obviously looking for something that would incriminate him.''

"Maybe. Maybe not.'' Frank gazed at me with infuriating blandness.

"But—but—what—I mean . . .'' I stammered to a standstill, glaring at him.

"Duchat could have had something incriminating on anyone,'' Frank said placidly. "Once he was dead, anyone might want to find it before we do. Could be someone who definitely didn't want Duchat dead, at least not until they found whatever they were looking for.''

"Frank?'' The detective was down on one knee. Frank went over to him, followed by Adam and me. He pointed to a dark splotch on the carpet. "More over there,'' he said, indicating several other spots in a trail toward the door.

Frank nodded. "Check it out.''

"What?'' I asked. "What is it? It's blood, isn't it?''

"We don't know,'' he said. "We'll find out. Now . . .''

"You see?'' I said. "Maybe Traci was attacked. Maybe she was kidnapped. Maybe . . .''

"Maybe it isn't blood,'' Frank growled. "Maybe it's someone else's blood. Get a hold of yourself, Gen.''

Adam eyed me smugly, and I frowned at him.

"Well, anyway,'' I said, "there are some other people who could have killed him. People who had more reason than Traci, and who are big enough to do the job without getting up on a ladder.''

Frank sighed. "Okay. What's the scoop?''

I laid out the various tidbits we had come up with, pleased to see that he took notes.

When I had run down, he stretched and yawned. "Okay. We appreciate the info. Actually, we knew about most of it, but you never know when a little piece might pull things together.''

I felt a little deflated, and I could feel an "I told you so'' waiting to emerge from Adam.

"Honest, Gen, we're not determined to pin this on your

little Traci,'' Frank said. ''If she's innocent, fine, I'll be happy for you.''

''I know,'' I said, but not happily.

''Now, don't think we don't appreciate all this,'' he said. ''But we would much rather do the detective work ourselves. Don't want any more bodies turning up, you see.''

I could feel my face turning red. ''I'd hardly call it detective work—'' I began, but he interrupted.

''Whatever you call it, it's dangerous, Gen. If you make the wrong person mad, you could be in big trouble. I can't keep you from talking to people, but I'd really like to think you'd use some common sense.''

''Well, of course I will,'' I declared. ''It's just—well, when you run into someone you know, it's natural to talk about anything exciting that's going on. And after all, a murder is pretty exciting, you must admit.''

''Mmmm,'' he murmured, cocking an eyebrow at me. ''Just don't go around looking for people to run into. And don't get in our way. Well-meaning people sometimes mess up an investigation. And that is really annoying, Gen.''

''I'm sure,'' I said meekly. ''I'll go and sin no more.''

Adam whistled cheerfully as he drove me home. It was in lieu of saying ''I told you so,'' and it was no improvement.

Chapter Fifteen

Traci still hadn't turned up by Wednesday morning. Sister Madonna called an assembly where she put her considerable talents to work reassuring the girls, and led us in a prayer for Miss Beaupré's safety and well-being. Then she went back to her office to deal with the parents who had begun calling. In the faculty lounge, Sarah reported that a number of parents were growing a little twitchy at the possibility that their children were in the hands of murderers. I suppose you couldn't blame them.

Such teaching as went on at St. Phil's that day would not have won any awards. The most you could say about it was that it took up some time. Rita Carstairs and Lucy Bennett were having their fifteen minutes of fame, and their peril grew with each retelling of the tale. Donald Tomcyk looked like a man who had been set upon by wolves. Ellen was worried about Traci enough to forget herself and begin speaking to me again.

And I was too distracted to put my heart into a scowl at my sophomores when they turned into a seething mass of hormones as Mr. Tomcyk himself entered the classroom that afternoon.

Sharon Cromwell had called to say we could pick up the works we had on exhibit. Would I, once again, drive the second van? I would. Donald left, taking with him the hearts of my Phillies, and I gave in to exhaustion, letting the girls spend the remaining fifteen minutes writing in their journals. I could easily imagine what they were writing about.

I had no intention of playing detective again. The truth was that I had been a little frightened by our visit with Clint Madison. All right, a lot frightened. Also, I did not want to be yelled at anymore. So I had no plans to do anything other than pick up paintings and sculptures and vamoose.

I don't know how to explain it. All I know is, there was Sharon Cromwell, and there was I, and we were exchanging polite pleasantries, and Donald was taking paintings down, and then an evil genie took possession of my mouth.

"By the way," I said, "you never mentioned that you had known Mark Duchat for a long time."

A visible shock went through her, and her face went white. "I—I . . ."

"When we talked to you on Monday," I said, "I got the impression that you hardly knew him. But Victor Ingle says that you knew him very well."

She lifted her chin. "Victor Ingle might say almost anything," she said. "Since he certainly had reasons to want Mark dead, reasons that the police undoubtedly are aware of. He's simply trying to point fingers away from himself."

"Clint Madison says you knew Duchat pretty well, too," I said.

Sharon sat down on a bench and clasped her hands. She shook her head, then smiled grimly. "Well, then I guess it's no secret, is it? It isn't something I'm fond of remembering, however. By now you must know enough about Mark to realize he was no Prince Charming."

"No argument."

"All right. I did know him, years ago. We were art students in Pittsburgh. He was good, I was so-so. I always thought he could have become a fine artist, but he hadn't the desire to work at it. The only art he really cared for was the art of the con, and he was very good at that."

She moved to a table containing a coffee urn.

"Would you like a cup?" I declined, and she poured a cup for herself, came back, and sat on the bench.

"He was also handsome, charming, romantic, and always broke," she continued. "I was, as the romance novels used to put it, swept off my feet." She made a face. "I won't bore you with details. I believed we were going to be married. So, of course, there was nothing wrong with his borrowing a little money from me for his last year of school. The next thing I knew, he was gone, and so was my four thousand dollars, the remnant of my savings account."

I could see why she had been reluctant to noise that around. It was embarrassing. Then again, it was hardly worth killing for.

"He left two steps ahead of the police," she said. "I was not the only one who had been hoodwinked. There were some questions about stolen artworks, as well."

"I'm sorry," I said. "I shouldn't have . . ."

She laughed shortly. "The next time I saw him was in Paris, and he had a new name and a new career."

"A new name?"

She smiled at me. "Oh, yes, I knew him before he was Mark Duchat. In those days he was Paul Cataline, art student. In Paris, he had become Mark Duchat, art dealer. Eventually I found out that he had left New York in something of a hurry. Dealing in stolen artworks, I heard. Hence the new name. Even that was a game, so typical of him. He just couldn't resist cuteness."

I shook my head, confused. "How do you mean, a game?"

"You know a little French, don't you? *Du chat* means . . ."

"Of the cat," I said.

She nodded. "Mark Duchat, mark of the cat. It was the kind of thing he found amusing, teasing the police who were looking for Paul Cataline. When he showed up in Derry, I really thought he had reformed. He had a legitimate position as a critic. I didn't catch on to his new game until last year. Apparently I'm a slow learner."

"He seems to have charmed a lot of women," I said.

"Oh, indeed. Not all of them are stupid enough to be charmed twice, however. I should have warned Traci about him, but I suspected warnings would have fallen on deaf ears, especially since I was the woman scorned, so to speak." She laughed without humor. "I know that's what Traci thought about Omega."

"Omega Starlight? The artist?" I asked. Right, as if there might be two Omegas in the general area. "She was one of his conquests, too?"

"Long enough to get him introductions to some of the flightier patrons of the arts," Sharon said. "And to get her into enough compromising positions that she preferred to keep from her husband."

"Blackmail, too?" Was there no end to the man's talents? I wondered.

Sharon smiled. "Oh, nothing so crude! Just a delicate suggestion or two. Omega's husband has piles of money, which he uses generously to indulge her artistic endeavors, and nothing she does is so outlandish as to make him tighten the purse strings. But—he is as jealous as he is rich, and an affair would have ended the marriage. And, of course, there was a prenuptial agreement."

"Marvelous," I murmured. "Listen, Sharon . . ." I hesitated, wondering how far I could push this. She watched me warily. "Something Victor Ingle said . . . well, did Duchat really agree to take the blame for the fake paintings?"

She took so long to answer that I was about to think she wouldn't. Finally she sighed. "No. Of course not. Paul—Mark never took responsibility for anything. He told me he had nothing to do with it. It was between me and Victor, he said. Victor brought the paintings to me; I sold them as legitimate works. He had the records to prove it. And of course, he would have whatever records he needed." She shrugged and threw up her hands. "I don't have anything else to tell you. Don't know why I told you any of it, as a matter of fact. It's just . . . well, the police will know all about it anyway, if they don't already. So what's the difference?'' She stared at me, her eyes hard. ''I didn't kill him, believe it or not.''

I wasn't sure whether I believed her, but I wanted to. I thought she was more of a victim than any of the suspects, except for Traci, of course.

Donald had the things gathered and was loading them into the vans, and Sharon Cromwell was only too glad to see me go. I helped get everything secured and we delivered our cargo to the school, where Mr. Merryman was waiting with his customary lack of pleasure at seeing us. Since he, Sister Madonna, and Sarah were the only ones who had keys to get into the building, he had no choice.

''Sister wants all this back behind the stage till the girls pick 'em up,'' he said. ''Of course, I'm the one has to find space for 'em. Sister never thinks about that, does she?''

He glared at me, and I obediently shook my head.

''Take all this stuff back there, track slush through my clean halls. No one cares about that, though.'' Grumbling, he helped stack the shrouded paintings and sculptures on carts and we wheeled them down his clean halls to the auditorium. There he dismissed us, and we went back to put the vans in the lot.

Donald hadn't had much to say all afternoon. I supposed he was worried about Traci. I tried to make conversation, but I received only monosyllables in response until we were outside.

''Were you talking to Sharon Cromwell about the murder?'' Donald asked suddenly. ''I'm sorry—I didn't mean to eavesdrop, but I couldn't help hearing some of it.''

''No apology needed,'' I said. ''I was just trying to find out who might have done Duchat in. I keep hoping something will click, something to prove Traci didn't do it.'' I gave him a brief synopsis of Sharon's story.

He looked interested. ''Do you think the cops know about all that?''

''I don't know. Probably. But they're so sure Traci did

it, even after her apartment was ransacked. They think she faked that, because there's no evidence of forced entry. Or else that someone other than the killer may be trying to find something."

"That's crazy."

"Donald," I said, "have you heard from Traci?"

His head jerked and he stopped dead for just a second. "Why would I have heard from her?"

"I don't know. I just wondered. I mean, I don't understand why she'd run away, but if she did, I thought she might get in touch with someone. She didn't call me, or Ellen, or Sister Madonna. I just—I was hoping you might know where she is."

Donald turned his face away from me and began to walk faster. "No. Sorry, but I can't tell you anything. Traci and I weren't—weren't—you know, since she met Duchat . . ."

"I know, Donald. I'm sorry."

He nodded quickly and strode away. I watched him go, feeling an unhappy tingling somewhere inside.

He was lying. I'd bet a month of hot fudge sundaes on it.

Chapter Sixteen

"So what are you saying?" Ellen examined another photocopy, okayed it, and added it to the stack on her desk. "You think Donald kidnapped Traci, or what?"

"I don't know. All I'm saying is that he lied about not knowing where Traci is."

She frowned at me. "Don't you think you might be jumping to conclusions, Gen? Donald's twitchy, but so are the rest of us. It isn't every day that someone you know just vanishes. When you're worried, sometimes you don't act normal."

True enough. Even Sister Madonna was looking a little frazzled by Thursday, with uncharacteristic worry lines on her serene brow. Bernadette Melendez had committed the unpardonable sin of yelling at Mr. Merryman for locking up the softball equipment; we would all do penance for that, it was clear. In freshman religion class, Sister Charlotte had forgotten the corporal works of mercy. The Phillies were so wired they almost twanged. A few more days and St. Philomena's would self-destruct.

I didn't know what I thought. It was ridiculous, I told myself, to imagine that Donald would do anything to hurt Traci.

Ellen put another copy on the pile. "The thing to do is just find something to get your mind off this for a while," she advised. "How about going to Engelhart's after school? They're having a sale on sweaters."

"Can't," I said. "I—um—have something to do."

She squinted at me suspiciously. ''Something important enough to pass up a sale on lamb's wool?''

I felt myself blushing. ''I have to pick up my VCR,'' I said. Which was true; I did have to pick it up, just not that day.

''You're going to go detecting again,'' she said. ''You are, aren't you?''

''Don't be silly.'' I laughed, a false laugh if I ever heard one, and she glared at me. I ducked out and escaped before she could say more, and managed to avoid her for the rest of the day.

The thing was, I really couldn't help myself. The news reports had said a knife had been found at the gallery, and I could guess which knife that was and whose fingerprints were on it. And, as if in counterpoint, that morning there had been a ''Community Events'' notice in the *Sentinel,* to the effect that Omega Starlight was having a show at a small downtown gallery. I hadn't been looking for it, it just jumped out at me. Which would indicate that it was a sort of sign from—well, perhaps not from God; I thought it might be just as well not to presume—but at least from fate.

Surely it wouldn't hurt to check her out. If she turned out to be four feet tall and consumptive, we could probably rule her out. I was not enthusiastic about going alone, but I had an unfortunate lack of willing sidekicks at that point.

I found the gallery lurking between a vaguely threatening coffeehouse and a store specializing in books advocating various sorts of revolution. I parked in the alley beside the coffeehouse, squeezing in between a red MG and a multi-colored 1972 Ford Pinto, and was greeted at the gallery door by a solemn young man who gave me a brochure and pointed me toward a doorway hung with beads.

There was a small group of people gathered in a dim room, gazing expectantly at a raised platform, and I sat and gazed likewise. A creature covered with hair sat on the floor at one side, playing a reedy dirge on some sort of flute.

After allowing sufficient time for the audience to become suffused with gloom, a woman whose head erupted with wild red hair sprang onto the stage. She wore a black caftan and carried a dead chicken by its neck.

"Omega!" I jumped as the sepulchral voice boomed from some unknown region.

"Omega!" Voices from the audience repeated solemnly.

An electric fan droned into life behind Omega, fluttering her caftan. Holding the forlorn chicken in front of her, she proceeded to pluck its feathers and fling them into the air, to be blown over the rapt audience. As a finale she tossed the naked bird into our midst, a ploy that met with applause and further chanting of "Omega!"

After that, things sort of blurred together as I tried to imagine what I was supposed to be getting from this. Well, I like to be a good sport. This was the kind of thing that got awards from the NEA, after all, and I like to think I'm getting something for my money. Also, I hated to have to admit that Mark Duchat and I might have had something in common.

My wandering attention returned to the stage with a jolt as Omega stepped to the front, holding a knife in both hands. If she started tossing knives into the audience . . .

She didn't. Instead, she plunged the knife into her chest and . . . *No, no,* I assured my fibrillating heart. She stuck it into her caftan, and slit the garment all the way down, revealing Omega covered with feathers. Shrugging off the sleeves, she then proceeded to pluck said feathers, which were much larger than those of the unfortunate chicken. Omega's devotees cooed with delight as they collected the floating souvenirs. I, on the other hand, was busily calculating possible trajectories should the artist plan to fling her own carcass at us.

It became clear to me that I had fallen into a cult of the seriously deranged, and I began to plan my escape. But, as all good things must come to an end, so did the performance. Standing before us at last au naturel, Omega shook out a king-sized black plastic trash bag, stepped into it, and drew it up slowly over her head. She pulled the drawstring to close the opening and slowly crumpled to the floor as the lights went out.

On balance, I decided I liked Clint Madison's work better.

In a moment the lights came up again, revealing an empty stage, onto which stepped a small, insubstantial man who informed us that we were welcome to view Omega Starlight's paintings in the next room.

I wasn't sure I was up to that. However, in for a penny, in for a pound, so I directed my reluctant feet toward the display, following my fellow art lovers.

I didn't find what I expected, although heaven knows what I expected. The paintings were rather engaging, as a matter of fact: mainly abstracts, some watercolor or pencil, but mostly acrylics. She had also done some mobiles, which were another thing. As a personal quibble, I'm about as fond of mobiles as I am of mimes, which is to say, not very.

Anyway, I was moseying along, enjoying the paintings, when I bumped into another viewer.

"Oh, sorry," I said. "I—oh!"

I was looking into the face of Victor Ingle, who was just as startled as I.

"Mrs. . . . Galway, is it? We meet again." He didn't sound at all pleased.

"Oh, yes! We do! This is a surprise!" I blithered.

He smiled ironically. "You're a fan of Omega's?" he asked.

"Yes, indeed! Oh, yes. Yes." I must do something about my vocabulary skills, I decided. "And you?"

"I'm a dealer," he said, raising an eyebrow. "Tell me, Mrs. Galway, is Omega on your list?"

"List?" I cursed my propensity for blushing as I felt my face lighting up again. Ingle's lips curled in a mocking smile. *Oh, what the heck,* I thought. "As a matter of fact, she is, Mr. Ingle. It's a fairly long list, of course. A surprising number of people seem not to have wished Mark Duchat well.''

''True. That doesn't necessarily lead to murder, however.''

''Sharon Cromwell did lie, by the way,'' I said. ''About Duchat's agreeing to take responsibility for selling the forgeries.''

''As I said.''

''Yes. She says he told her she'd have to take it up with you, since you were the dealer.''

''And I have risen to the top of your list again?''

''Not the top. Not the bottom, either.''

He sighed. ''Just an also-ran, eh? Well, my dear lady, I wouldn't want to upset your clever little scenarios. But I do feel I would be remiss if I neglected to mention a suspect that you seem to be missing entirely.''

''And that would be?''

''Have you even considered Mark's ex-partner?''

''Ex-partner?''

''From his dealership in New York.''

''That was a long time ago, wasn't it?''

''When your partner lands you in prison and then runs off with your money, you might find it hard to forgive and forget. And if he's disappeared by the time you get out of prison, it might take a while to track him down.''

''You think his partner found him here?''

He laughed. ''I haven't the least idea. I never knew the man, wouldn't know him if he were standing beside me. It just seems to me that all of you detectives are overlooking one person who would have a very strong motive. Revenge, Mrs. Galway.''

His eyes focused over my left shoulder. ''Well, here is our artist.''

I turned. It took a few seconds before I recognized Omega Starlight. The electric hair was gone, replaced by a long black braid. She wore a voluminous chiffon dress of emerald green.

Ingle introduced us, then bowed to me. "I'll leave you to do whatever it is you plan to do," he said. "Just a word of friendly warning, though. Remember what curiosity did to the cat. And you do not have nine lives, Mrs. Galway."

We watched him go, Omega frowning slightly.

"Peculiar man," she said, and turned her attention to me, impaling me with catlike eyes. "You are interested in my work?"

With difficulty I wrested my thoughts from Ingle's last comments. "Uh, yes. I like these paintings. The acrylics especially."

She gazed at the walls as if surprised to see the items hanging there. "One of my moods," she said vaguely. "I've moved on from there."

I wasn't sure what response might be considered appropriate, so I contented myself with nodding wisely. "You had a show at the Cromwell Gallery, didn't you?"

"Yes." She looked at me. "Did you attend?"

I shook my head. "I read the review by Mark Duchat," I said. "He was not very kind."

"A Philistine," she said, waving a dismissive hand. "I pay no attention to reviews. Especially reviews by barbarians such as Mark Duchat. His opinions are not in my consciousness."

I hesitated, considering the one life I had to risk for curiosity. However, Omega Starlight didn't look dangerous. "I understand you were a little upset when you went to see him at his office, though. You . . ."

"I am an artist," she said. "I have certain sensitivities. When my art is derided by vulgarians, it is natural that I experience some anger. But it was nothing. He is nothing. The whole thing was another part of my life."

I took a shot in the dark. "Why were you at the Cromwell Gallery the night Duchat was killed?"

She stared at me, her eyes slits. "Not to see him, I assure

you. I had canceled him from my mind before then. I went to the gallery to collect a painting I had left to be framed.'' She tilted her head to one side and smiled suddenly. ''You want to know if I killed him? Certainly not! He was not worth killing!''

Her eyes were not smiling at all. My interest in self-preservation was strongly advising me to let it go. Naturally, I ignored it.

''There is some talk that Duchat was more than a critic to you,'' I said. ''That you and he were closer than your husband knew.''

The smile vanished. ''There are always rumors. If such a thing were true, of course, I would be even less likely to have killed him. One would not know if certain information would come to light in such a case.''

''Of course,'' I murmured.

''I knew Mark Duchat in another part of my life,'' she said. ''It is no longer relevant. I have forgotten it. You should perhaps do the same. It would be more comfortable.''

I agreed and bade her a hasty adieu. I seemed to have been threatened twice in the last half hour, something of a record, surely.

Chapter Seventeen

A black Lincoln was following me. I noticed it at the first corner after leaving the gallery, and it stuck with me all the way down Walloon Street, left onto Linden, right onto Camden. Victor Ingle's bulletin about curiosity versus cats kept running through my mind like a commercial for a fast-food place. Occasionally the refrain was interrupted by a voice whining, *See? Everybody told you to stay out of it. But would you? Oh, no! Well, now you've done it, and I hope you're happy!*

I wasn't happy, though. I took a squealing left at Munsen, darted around a truck whose driver was about to make a turn and who shook a fist at me, went through the parking lot at Safeway, and fled down an alley, coming out on Beacon. My Escort and I both breathed a sigh of relief as we made tracks home.

I pulled into the parking lot and sat for a minute or two, until my heart stopped thumping. It was just starting to rain, and I wrapped my scarf around my head and made a dash around the house toward the front porch. I was halfway there when the Lincoln glided to a parking space at the curb. I ran for the front steps, hearing behind me the slam of a car door and footsteps that sounded as if they belonged to a large, vicious man.

With the speed induced by panic, I sprinted across the porch and reached for the doorknob. An arm stretched past me and—

"Allow me," the large, vicious man said, pushing the door open and holding it for me.

93

"Erggh," I answered, dashing through and running to the elevator, which was standing open, by a rare stroke of good fortune. I ducked in.

And was followed, of course, by the large, vicious man. I was busy berating myself for stupidity beyond the call of duty when the doors slid shut. He would naturally prefer to kill me in the seclusion of an elevator. He looked like a neat, tidy man, not given to making a mess in public places.

He smiled. "You're in the front apartment on two, aren't you?"

"Mmmm," I said, trying to remember how to scream, in the event that I was still alive when the elevator door opened, assuming that I was to be killed in the comfort of my own apartment. "Yes. My husband and I. He'll be waiting for me. He's a police officer."

The large, vicious man pressed the button. "Really." Did he look impressed? Nervous? "I've seen you a few times when I've come to visit my mother," he said. "She's in the rear apartment. Ruth Shelby."

"Mrs. Shelby. Of course. Why yes," I gibbered. "How nice to finally meet you, Mr . . . ?"

"Shelby," he said. "Jack Shelby."

We reached the second floor and went our separate ways, he to ask his mother whether she thought she was entirely safe with neighbors who were clearly unstable, I to slump on my sofa and give myself a lengthy lecture on paranoia and generally embarrassing behavior.

After I got tired of listening to that I poured myself a large glass of wine and communed with my infernal answering machine.

Sister Madonna wanted to know if I'd heard anything from Traci.

Carol Donahue, who rented my house in Beaverbrook, informed me that the garbage disposal had died.

Adam said he had a good deal on a printer to replace my horse-and-buggy one.

Ellen ordered me to call if I was not yet murdered.

There was no message from Nora; I wondered if she was sick.

I dutifully returned the calls: No, there was no word from Traci. Call Mr. Lemmon, the plumber. Get the printer. Of course I'm not murdered, don't be ridiculous, I just went to look at some paintings, and incidentally I met a very nice man who visits his mother on my floor.

And then I sat and considered what I had learned, which had pretty much fled my mind while I faced death.

So. Omega Starlight was either a space cadet, or not. I had the feeling that she could be hazardous to one's health. Still, I wasn't sure I saw her killing because of a bad review or a soured affair.

I was more than ever convinced that Victor Ingle was a dangerous man. If Duchat had planned to throw him to the wolves, he could have been angry enough to hit first and think about it later. And obviously Duchat was capable of betraying a partner, since he had apparently done it before.

Ah, yes! At last I remembered what I had been groping through my brain for. Duchat had had a partner in his former business. A partner who had gone to prison, while Duchat took his money and went off to Paris to be reborn.

It still seemed farfetched that this partner had located Duchat under a new name in a new place with a new career. But it was a much better idea than seeing Traci as the culprit. It was at least worth a little investigation.

Annie was just back from Maine. I had expected to get her answering machine, and took it as a good sign when she answered in person. I brought her up to date on the case, not that there was a lot to tell, since I felt it inadvisable to mention my own activities. I have noticed that grown children are prone to disapprove of many of their parents' hobbies.

''Anyhow,'' I said, ''now I hear that Mark Duchat had a partner in his art dealership in New York. The rumor is that they were involved in art theft, and that the partner took the blame and went to prison. Also that Duchat went off to Europe with all the funds.''

''Nice,'' Annie said.

''Yes. It occurred to me that you might be able to find out what happened, and where the partner is today.''

''Probably. At least I can find out about the business and what happened to it. If there was a crime involved, I ought to be able to find out who went to jail.''

''That'd be a help,'' I said. ''If you can get the partner's name, and even better, if you can find out what he looked like.''

''Should be news photos. I'll see what I can find out.''

''Thanks, hon. But—be careful, okay?''

''Excuse me? What am I to be careful about?''

''Well, I don't know. Probably nothing. Clear off in New York . . . I mean, if the partner is there, it's pretty clear that he wasn't the killer. But . . .''

She sighed. ''Of course, he could have killed and returned by now. Very motherly you are, I must say!''

''Oh, my gosh! I hadn't thought of that!'' Terror and guilt flooded over me. ''Forget the whole thing! Do not ask anyone anything!''

''Too late, mums.'' Annie laughed. ''You've got me curious now. I'm a reporter, you know?''

''No, no, no . . .''

''I will, however, be careful. And I'll let you know as soon as I find out anything. Cherry 'bye.''

''Annie, I forbid . . .''

She had hung up. *Well, you've done it again,* my inner voice snarled. *What kind of mother are you?*

I fixed a TV dinner for myself. It was all I deserved.

Chapter Eighteen

"Jane Austen had a genius for making the commonplace interesting," I said. "She knew her own world well, and the very ordinary people who inhabited it. She liked those people, with all their good and bad points, so she was able to get inside their heads."

I could see that Jane and I had little in common today, as I was not having any luck at all in making the commonplace interesting, even to myself. Murder is not a good educational device, a fact we should all file away in case someday a group of experts decides to advocate it.

Still, education is expected to take place in a school, regardless of any distractions the outside world throws in its path. "The popular reading when Jane was young was dazzling romance. Not unlike our current era, as a matter of fact. Jane read those stories, but instead of being enthralled, she found them hilarious. When she was still a schoolgirl, she was writing spoofs of that kind of story." I paused and gazed at the rows of sad young faces before me. These were usually bright and vibrant young women, absorbing information almost before I could dish it out, and competing to toss questions, opinions, and interpretations back at me.

Peggy Rinaldi raised a tentative hand and I nodded at her. "Isn't that one of the big differences between Jane Austen and George Eliot?" she said, but not as though her heart was in it. "Austen puts more humor in her books, and Eliot—Eliot . . ." She sighed. "I forgot what my point was."

"Mrs. Galway?" Rita's voice sounded small. "Do you think . . . that . . . that Miss Beaupré . . . Do you think she's—she's . . ." Her voice trailed away and lost itself in the surrounding murmurs.

Lucy picked up the ball. "Do you think she's—dead, Mrs. Galway?"

"Of course not!" My voice was louder than I intended, and I could see growing fear on the girls' faces. The kids knew whistling past the graveyard when they heard it. "No," I said more quietly. "There isn't any reason to suspect that at all."

"We're getting a sub for French," Rita said.

"Well, of course," I said. "We can't just leave your class dangling. When Miss Beaupré returns, you'd be so far behind you'd never catch up by the end of term."

"If she returns," Peggy said.

"And if she isn't, you know, dead," Lucy said. "The news says she's suspected of being the killer."

A flurry of indignant denials rained around us, and I gave the desk a rather firm whack with my ruler to get their attention.

"Look, girls, I know this is hard. Everything's up in the air, and it's frustrating. Dead authors don't seem important in the circumstances, but we need to give them our attention now. It's a lot better than spending our time imagining the worst."

Rita sighed. "Sister Madonna says we have to have faith."

"Sister Madonna is right," I said.

"It's easier if you're a nun," Lucy said.

"Well, it shouldn't be," I said. "Work on it, Lucy. And in the meantime . . ."

"Pride and Prejudice," Peggy said.

Little by little they waded into the travails of the rich and famous of yesteryear. By the time the period ended it was almost like a normal class.

Unfortunately, each class was a rerun, and I was glad to

flee to the lounge at lunchtime, Sisyphus reprieved for an hour. The huddled masses that awaited me there looked as exhausted as I felt.

Actually, Donald looked much worse, more rumpled than usual. Sarah and Ellen wore dark circles under their eyes, and even Bernadette was low on verve. The nuns had deserted us, trooping off to the convent for lunch.

I unwrapped my sandwich (turkey, lettuce, low-fat mayo) and carrot sticks and contemplated them with little pleasure.

"At least the kids get to blame their mothers for crummy lunches," I said. "What kind of food is this for a person involved in a crisis?"

Ellen examined it. "What's wrong with it?"

"It isn't a Quarter-Pounder with cheese, that's what's wrong with it. It isn't french fries. It isn't a Snickers bar."

"It isn't a heart attack," Ellen said. "You'll live longer."

"So they say." I sighed and began to munch. "By the way, we have another suspect."

Everyone sat up and looked at me, Ellen with a suspicious squint.

"Mark Duchat had a business partner in New York," I said. "Apparently there was some criminal activity, and the partner got left holding the bag. Went to prison . . ."

"That was a long time ago, though, wasn't it?" Sarah gave me a puzzled frown.

"True. But if he was in prison, and by the time he got out, Duchat was gone, it could have taken a while to find him."

Donald looked the tiniest bit cheered up, but he was the only one. Sarah and Bernadette wore looks of doubt, and Ellen was still squinty-eyed.

"Where did you hear all this?" she asked.

Curses! I took a large bite of sandwich, searching for a plausible answer that wouldn't get me yelled at. Nothing came to mind.

"Well," I said, after chewing thoroughly and swallowing, only to find that she was still waiting for an answer, "as a matter of fact, Victor Ingle told me. He thought it would be helpful . . ."

"I knew it!" She glared at me. "You went to see that man again. You promised, and—"

"I did not promise. Not exactly. And anyhow, I didn't go to see him again. As it happens, I ran into him quite by accident."

"Oh? And where was that?"

"Downtown."

"Downtown where? You might as well tell me, Gen. I'll get it out of you sooner or later."

She would, too. "I was strolling through an art gallery," I said. "Not an unusual activity, you must agree. And suddenly, there he was . . ."

"What art gallery?" Good grief, the woman was inexorable! Her eyebrows shot up. "You went poking around after that woman, didn't you? Omega What's-her-face?"

"I wasn't poking anywhere, Ellen," I said, sitting up straight and looking, I hoped, dignified. "I simply wanted to see what sort of artist she was. I'm interested in that sort of thing, you know."

She harrumphed. "Sure, sure. And is she the kind of artist who kills people, do you think?"

A little shiver ran down my back. "Actually," I said slowly, "I wouldn't be surprised."

There was a collective intake of breath. Before they had drawn all the air into their lungs, the door opened and Sister Madonna came in.

"I'm sorry to interrupt your lunch," she said. "I just wanted to tell Miss Joplin that I'll be out of the office for about an hour. I have to meet Miss Beaupré's parents when they arrive from New York." She sighed and shook her head. "Those poor people! I had hoped we would have some good news for them by now. Having their daughter missing for over three days must be torture for them."

Sister M. went on her errand, and we sat in gloomy silence for a few minutes.

''Do you think Traci was kidnapped?'' Bernadette asked. We all looked at one another unhappily.

''Maybe she ran away,'' Ellen said. ''If she saw someone was in her apartment, she might have been so scared . . .''

''But why wouldn't she come to one of us?'' I asked. ''If she was frightened, surely she'd want to go to someone who would help.''

''Maybe she did,'' Ellen said. ''She has other friends, after all. I'll bet she's staying with one of them until she gets her nerve up.''

''I hope,'' I said. I couldn't help thinking about the spots on the carpet. I wondered if Frank Monroe would tell me whether they had turned out to be blood. I had decided not to mention the stains to anyone else; people were worried enough as it was.

Chapter Nineteen

M r. Merryman poked his frosty head around the door frame and looked at me disapprovingly.

"You going to be very long, Miz Galway?"

I know better than to stay Mr. Merryman from his rounds. "Not long, Mr. Merryman. But you go ahead. I'll let myself out."

"Well, be sure the door locks after you," he grumbled, and detached himself from the doorway.

I was in Traci's classroom, searching through her French Lit books. I had remembered *Fleurs du Mal* as a French work by Baudelaire. If Duchat was playing tricks, I reasoned, the peculiar Ste. Thérèse could be a clue pointing to the poem. A clue to what, I had no idea, but my curiosity was whetted.

Unfortunately, I seemed to have wandered down a false trail. I found four books on Traci's shelves that had all or part of Baudelaire's long poem, but as far as I could see, none of them had any secret messages.

As I put the books back on the shelf, I heard one of the outside doors close, and I chastised myself for dillydallying. If I'd been just a few minutes quicker I could have gone out with Mr. M., instead of which I now had to go all the way around to the auditorium door, since that was the only one for which we mere teachers had keys to let ourselves out. Ah well.

The hall was dark except for the exit sign at either end, since Mr. M. does not believe in wasting electricity to light the way for tardy teachers. I shifted my purse and my tote bag to my left arm, pulled the classroom door shut, and groped for my key ring.

I don't know if it was a sound or a movement. Something too subtle to recall pulled my attention to the left, down the shadowy hall.

Someone stood there, almost at the end of the hallway, motionless and almost invisible. I nearly convinced myself that it was my imagination. But not quite.

''Who's there?'' I asked, proving once again that a college education does not necessarily make a person smarter. Not surprisingly, the lurker didn't sing out with his name. He started toward me.

I dropped my keys, backed into the overhead projector cart, grabbed the cart, and shoved it as hard as I could toward the dark figure. Then I ran for the auditorium door.

Which I would not be able to use, since I no longer had my keys.

Cursing under my breath, I dashed for the stairs, through the fire door, yanked off my shoes, dropped one on the first step of the down staircase, and tossed the other one a few steps down. I started up the stairs, for good measure flinging my tote bag over the railing. Then I proved to myself that I could still run up two steps at a time, although it would not be something that I cared to do on a regular basis.

I spun around the pillar at the top of the flight and flattened myself against the wall, gripping the handrail. If my pursuer didn't follow my red herrings downstairs, I promised myself, he would be surprised when he came around my corner. I flexed my knee, visualizing the proper placement for an efficient kick. Not a perfect plan, but at least it would give me a chance. All things considered, a lot better than getting trapped on the second floor, where there was no exit even if one did have a key.

I had hardly stationed myself, thanking God and Mr. Merryman for the dim lighting, when the fire door opened. Still panting a little, I stifled myself with my scarf, and after a second or two, I heard the footsteps going down.

It wouldn't take him long to discover I wasn't down there, though. I knew Mr. M. would have locked up the supply rooms and work areas, so there weren't many places my pursuer would have to look.

I ran down to the first floor and headed again for the exit. And remembered again that my stupid keys were somewhere on the floor by Traci's classroom door. I said a few words I hadn't used since I was young and vulgar and flung myself on hands and knees, feeling for the darned key ring that had certainly seemed plenty big enough before now. I would buy a key-finder if I lived long enough.

Time flies. In just no time at all I heard the fire doors open. Still on all fours, I crept into Traci's room, edged the door shut, and tried to conjure up a hiding place. Considering that this was the only unlocked door, and that it would not take a person of any intelligence very long to find the light switch beside the door, hiding did not seem a viable choice.

St. Philomena's is an old school. I had never thought of that as a particular benefit, but now I saw it as a part of God's plan. Because St. Phil's has actual windows that open, unlike its modern counterparts. Praising God and the bishop, I opened one of those windows and climbed up onto the sill. The ground was a bit farther away than I would have chosen if I were asked, but as the door opened behind me, the drop became much more appealing.

I slid through the opening, grabbed the sill, and dangled for a second or two, willing the ground to rise to my feet. Then I closed my eyes, let go, and in a very short time found myself in the mud and slush behind the privet hedges.

I cautiously moved each limb and decided I was intact. I began creeping along through the icy sludge behind the hedges, figuring that it would be wise to stay out of sight as long as possible. I was nearly to the end of the hedge when a pair of sneakers appeared under my nose. Dark trouser legs rose out of the sneakers.

"Urgh!" I said, jerking backward.

"Mrs. Galway? Is that you?"

I rocked back on my heels and peered up at Bridget Maguire. Clustered around her were Jean Ann, Denny, Kim, and Christy. They wore uniformly round eyes.

"Mrs. Galway?" Jean Ann said. "What are you doing?"

"Well!" I said. "This is a surprise. What are you doing here, girls?"

They looked at one another and back at me. The look asked me if I thought I was going to get away with the kind of response they used routinely with their parents. They were the experts, after all.

"We were coming from choir practice," Kim said politely.

"We saw something in the bushes," Bridget said.

They stood and waited patiently.

I sighed. "I was looking for—my earring. Yes, there it is! Thank goodness."

They regarded me with skepticism. Well, we do try to teach them to recognize fish stories.

I got up and brushed myself off, pulling the shreds of my dignity around me. "Time to be getting on home, girls. Your parents will be looking for you."

"Mrs. Galway, where are your shoes?" Denny asked.

We all examined my unshod feet while I considered possible explanations. It occurred to me that it might be good to leave the scene posthaste, and without getting the girls involved in something I didn't understand myself.

"I knew I forgot something," I said finally. "Well, they're locked in the school now. I guess they'll just have to stay there until Monday."

They looked at one another again, five pairs of eyebrows rising to their heights. I started walking briskly down the walk, urging them along with me. They were uncharacteristically silent, which I presumed meant they were busily assembling a dossier on me in their agile minds. It would at least provide something other than romance for their fevered brains to work on.

As if summoned by the thought, a familiar figure appeared around the side of the church, and I screeched to a stop, causing Kim to walk into me.

"Oh, look," Jean Ann whispered. "It's Mr. Tomcyk."

Indeed it was. Mr. Tomcyk hotfooting it along toward the parking lot. Mr. Tomcyk wearing dark jeans and a dark windbreaker.

Giggles and whispers indicated that I was off their list of wonders for the moment. We had reached the path leading to the convent, and I left the girls with a final admonition to go home and sauntered up to the door, aware of their eyes boring into my back.

Sister Charlotte answered the bell, and she blinked only a little at my muddy feet and the shrubbery in my hair before trotting away to fetch Sister Madonna and call the police.

We were still engaged in fruitless speculation when the police arrived, and it was clear that the officers were disappointed in our failure to suggest any reason why the intruder had come after me instead of simply escaping after being spotted. Particularly since we could find nothing missing in the school.

Sgt. Cassidy looked at me sadly as he asked, without much hope, if I could give any sort of description of the Shadow Man. I had to admit that I had been too interested in saving myself to pay strict attention to any identifying features of my pursuer. Mentioning that he was taller than I brought a polite silence which said more loudly than words that most adults are taller than I and that such things are relative.

I kept to myself the fact that I had seen Donald shortly after the main event, though I couldn't have said why. Certainly it was reasonable for Donald, or anyone else, to be walking on the street beside the church. There was something vaguely paranoid about jumping to the conclusion . . .

On the other hand, it wasn't the first time I'd had a flicker of suspicion about Donald.

After the police had looked around I retrieved my scattered belongings. Except for the keys. They had vanished.

Chapter Twenty

I spent Saturday morning sorting the papers that had flown every which way when I dumped my tote bag. Whatever else might be going on in the world, English papers must be read and corrected.

It was almost noon by the time I matched up all the pages, and I rewarded myself with a cup of raspberry tea and turned on the TV to catch the news. As on every day for the past three days, I hoped to hear some encouraging developments in the murder investigation, including the discovery that Traci was alive, well, and innocent.

"Police are questioning a colleague of a missing teacher," Corinne Massey said, wearing her combination pleasant/concerned look. "Traci Beaupré, a teacher at St. Philomena's High School, has been missing since Tuesday, after a break-in at her apartment. Last night police arrested fellow teacher Donald Tomcyk when he was found at the apartment. Tomcyk has made no statement as to why he was on the premises. It is believed he had a key, since there was no evidence of forced entry. Police believe Beaupré's disappearance may be connected with the recent murder of local art critic Mark Duchat. No arrests have been made in that case."

I sat and stared at the screen while Corinne and her side-kick William Ortner delivered various bits of news to people who cared.

This didn't make sense. I sifted through the mental files made up of information on Duchat's murder. Several people could be searching Traci's apartment, for the same reason they would have searched Duchat's—looking for records that might prove damaging in some way. Victor Ingle, certainly, who wouldn't want his shady dealings known. Sharon Cromwell might also be hurt if it was discovered that she had sold forged artworks. Omega Starlight didn't want her husband to find out how well she knew Duchat. And any of them might figure, since nothing was turned up in Duchat's apartment, that he could have left it in Traci's. Someone had already searched the place, in fact.

But what would Donald be looking for? He wasn't involved in the forgeries. Duchat wouldn't have any incriminating evidence for him to worry about. Donald had no reason to search Traci's apartment.

Unless.

I swallowed hard and tried to dismiss the thought, but it wouldn't go away.

Unless, it insisted, he had been there before. Unless he was afraid he had left something behind that someone, sooner or later, would connect to him. Unless he had been responsible for Traci's disappearance.

The phone rang.

"Mrs. Galway? Have you heard the news?" Sister Madonna sounded as shocked as I felt.

I took a deep breath. "Well, Sister, I think I may have some more bad news." I told her about seeing Donald at St. Phil's the night before. "It's just so hard to see Donald as a—a . . ."

She sighed. "I know. But I do think we must tell the police. It seems to me we owe it to Miss Beaupré. Of course, we must still pray that this is all a mistake."

"I'll go and see the police," I said, with considerable lack of enthusiasm, not having any reason to believe I'd be met with joy at the station.

"I think we should go together, Mrs. Galway. It does involve the school to some extent, after all."

I wasn't reluctant, since I hoped the average cop would be less likely to shout at a nun, and, by extension, at a person accompanied by a nun. It was worth a shot. I agreed to pick Sister up at the convent in half an hour.

It gave me time to answer calls from Ellen and Nora, both of whom seemed to think I would have an explanation for the new development, and from Adam, who hadn't heard the news, but who had news of his own: the stains on Traci's carpet were, indeed, blood.

I almost walked out on the next call, since I didn't feel up to discussing the whole thing again. But, deciding I might as well get it over with, I picked up the receiver and growled hello.

"Geneviève?" said a little voice, barely a whisper.

"Traci?" I shouted. "Traci, is that you? Where are you?"

"I am here at Donald's apartment. I have just heard on the television that Donald is arrested. But he did not do anything! I have to tell them."

"What in the world are you doing at his place? Have you been there all this time? What happened? What do you mean, he didn't do anything? What is . . ." I stopped for a breath.

"I—I—I," she stammered.

"Let's start over," I said. "No doubt you will tell me all these things as time goes on. For now, what's going on?"

"I have to tell the police that Donald did not burglar my apartment. He was helping me."

I am not fond of complications, and it occurred to me that there were far too many of them here. "Um—Traci, are you sure—well, I don't want to upset you, but—are you sure Donald is *helping* you?"

"Geneviève, what are you saying? Of course I am sure! He has saved me from the burglar. He has said I must stay hiding, because I do not know who attacked me. But now I have to go to the police. I do not want to call them to come here, because whoever is searching may see them and will then think Donald has something to search for. But I do not have my car, so . . .''

"I'll come and get you," I said.

I debated whether to call Sister Madonna and postpone our police appearance. If Donald really was one of the good guys, there was no reason to point our fingers at him. But I decided it was time for someone else to get dragged into this mess, and Madonna seemed a likely prospect.

"Plans have changed a bit, Sister," I informed her as she buckled up.

She raised inquiring eyebrows, and I relayed the latest development during our drive to Donald's apartment.

"Well!" She sounded remarkably cheerful under the circumstances. "That certainly puts a new light on things, doesn't it? Perhaps it was just as well that you didn't tell the police about your seeing Mr. Tomcyk. We wouldn't have wanted to cast suspicion on an innocent person."

It seemed to me that we had very quickly exonerated Mr. Tomcyk.

Traci was ready to go when we arrived, and if she was surprised to see Sister Madonna with me, she gave no sign. I insisted that Donald would survive for as long as it took to tell us the whole story, and Traci reluctantly agreed.

"On Tuesday night I went to have dinner with friends from Canterville," she began. "When I came home, everything was dark in my apartment. I am used to leaving a light on the timer, but I supposed it had burned out. But when I went inside, someone ran at me and pushed me so that I fell. I shouted, and then he hit me. And then he ran out."

"My heavens!" Sister said. "You poor child!"

"No idea who it was?" I asked.

She shook her head. "I fell and bumped my head, and I was stunned for a moment. Then I put on the light and I saw my books and papers were disarranged. Then I heard a noise and I was afraid someone was still there, so I ran out."

"And the blood got on your carpet when the man hit you?" I asked.

She looked puzzled for a moment. "Blood? I didn't know about it. But yes, I suppose. I struck my knee against a table, and it was bleeding."

"But, Miss Beaupré," Sister said, "why didn't you go to the police? Why did you run away? We've all been very worried, dear."

She looked abashed. "I am sorry, Sister. I was very afraid. I could see that person had been looking for something in my apartment. And that would mean he had not found what he wanted in Mark's apartment, so he thinks I must have it. I think, well, I have interrupted him, so he has maybe not yet found it. So he will come back."

"But the police . . ." I said.

"I know I should call them," she said. "I went downstairs to Mrs. Todd's, but she was not at home. The people next door, they were away also. And I was not thinking well, because I was still afraid. So then I went to your house, Geneviève."

I sighed. "And I wasn't home either."

"So I waited there for a while. Then I thought, well, I must go home, because the burglar will surely be gone, and I will call the police. But the police were already there. I thought they must have come to arrest me, because they would not know about the burglar. They have found the knife, and I think they do not believe how everything happened. So I think they will still think I am lying."

"Well, where in the world have you been since then?" I asked.

"I went to Donald's," she said. "I thought he would help me. And he did. He said we must try to think what it is that this person is looking for. If he believes it is something in my apartment, then it must be something Mark could have brought there. So I should be able to guess what it must be. Then I remembered the package Mark has left, so I thought it might be that."

"Makes sense," I said.

"Yes. That is why Donald was at my apartment, to get that package. It is my fault. I should have gone with him. But he said I must stay away from sight."

"We'll worry about Donald later," I said. "What's in the package?"

"Just a book about art collections and a book of poetry. I do not see why either would be important, but it was all I could think of. Mark was always making riddles. I thought perhaps there was something in those books that someone might want."

"It could be," I said.

"So," Sister said, "we must examine the books, don't you agree?"

"Possibly easier said than done," I said. "Considering that Donald was caught, you know. Evidently the police are still watching Traci's place."

"And I must go and ask that the police release Donald," Traci said.

"But," Sister Madonna said, "your parents are at your apartment now, Miss Beaupré. They called this morning to say they would be staying there. It would be only reasonable for you to go to them. And you can certainly call the police from there. And while we are waiting for them, Miss Beaupré would certainly be entitled to look at some of her books." She looked so guileless that it was almost hard to believe that she was suggesting obstruction of justice. And when I pointed out the possibility, she appeared genuinely shocked.

"Mrs. Galway, I am certainly not planning to withhold evidence from the police. In fact, we are hoping to find some helpful evidence, are we not? But we can hardly be said to withhold that which we have not yet found."

The convent's gain was surely the legal profession's loss. I was not about to argue with that logic.

At Traci's, we were met with tears and embraces from her parents. While the prodigal daughter explained herself to mère and père Beaupré, Sister and I politely directed our attention to the decor.

"This is an unusual picture of Ste. Thérèse," Sister said, frowning at the painting I had noticed on Tuesday. "Not very attractive."

I joined her. "I know. She looks sly, doesn't she? And those are certainly not roses she's holding. Not to mention that the inscription has nothing to do with the poor little saint."

"Nothing at all," Traci agreed, coming up behind us. "It is more of Mark's tricks and riddles, you see."

"What is it supposed to mean?" I asked.

She sighed. "I don't know. Mark gave it to me for my birthday. Ste. Thérèse is my namesake, you know. And it is good work, although I do not like it. Why he has written '*Les fleurs du mal*' I do not know. He laughs and says, 'Ah, Baudelaire holds the key to everything.' He says, 'You are the only one who knows this, but you don't know what you know.'"

"Good grief," I said. "Did he tell you why she's carrying tulips and African violets?"

Traci gave a small laugh. "Yes, but I did not then know why he found it amusing. The African violets, he said, are called *Saintpaulia*. And the other flowers, they are not tulips, they are called cat's ears."

"Paul Cataline." I groaned. "He did enjoy his little jokes, didn't he?"

Sister Madonna shook her head. "He spent a great deal of time and effort on such foolishness, it seems to me."

We examined the two books Duchat had left behind. As far as we could tell, there was nothing at all in them that could have accounted for anyone's interest.

We were still trying to imagine what the searcher could be looking for so determinedly when the police arrived.

Chapter Twenty-one

Frank Monroe was clearly not pleased to see me, and although he didn't exactly glare at Sister Madonna, he showed no happiness at her presence either. His partner, one Officer Breger, didn't know any of us well enough to dislike us, but I was sure he would learn quickly.

I couldn't tell whether they believed Traci's saga, but they did have to accept the idea that she had not been murdered, which wiped out one charge against Donald, at least. Given that Traci hadn't been charged with any crime, he couldn't be charged with harboring a fugitive, either. Of course, there was still the possibility of obstructing justice, a thought that caused a bit of a chill among the three of us, for obvious reasons.

At the moment, Frank was fixated on our presence here and now. How was it, he wanted to know, that Traci had called us before calling the police? Why had she come home, if she was frightened, instead of coming to the station?

I had noticed that police officers tend to be suspicious, a trait that probably stood them in good stead when they were dealing with criminals. When they were dealing with people such as us, however, it was tiresome, since it required our answering many more questions than we would have liked to.

It was handy having Sister Madonna as one of our group. Most police officers are uncomfortable attacking the credibility of nuns, even in these rather rude times, and it certainly seemed reasonable that Traci—young, scared, alone— would call on the person she saw as a bulwark.

Which did not explain my presence. A presence that was becoming much too present, if I caught his drift.

"Mrs. Galway drove, Sgt. Monroe. We have only one car at the convent, you see. And one of the other sisters was using it."

With bad grace, Frank accepted that. Miss Beaupré would be expected to come down and make a statement, he said. The sooner the better. Now would be good.

"But of course, Sergeant," Traci said. "I shall be happy to come. Poor Donald, he must be exonerated."

Frank raised an eyebrow and grumbled as Traci fetched her coat and purse. After she and her parents had left with the police, Sister and I sat down and looked at each other.

"Whatever is being sought obviously hasn't been found yet," Sister said finally. "I think we have to assume that was the object of the break-in at the school, don't you?"

"Unless you're a fan of coincidences," I agreed.

"Doesn't it seem reasonable that Mr. Duchat would keep his records easily accessible for himself? Probably in his apartment?"

"Yes," I said. "But someone searched his apartment, and apparently didn't find anything."

She nodded. "But, don't you see, Mrs. Galway, we may have some information that person didn't have? Mr. Duchat told Miss Beaupré that Baudelaire held the key. What might that suggest?"

"Maybe a real key? In a volume of *Fleurs du Mal.*

Maybe. If someone were just looking for records, letters, whatever . . ."

No wonder someone killed Duchat, I reflected. The man was darned annoying, with his stupid little games and riddles.

"We need to get into Mr. Duchat's apartment," Sister said, as calmly as she might have said, "We need to order new math textbooks," or, "We need to get the permanent records updated by next week."

"I beg your pardon?" I asked, thinking about the penalties for breaking and entering.

"There must be some reasonable errand that would take us there," she said, gazing at me expectantly.

I gazed back for a while, feeling as I used to when Professor Considine posed a question in philosophy class, and waited for eons while his chosen victim struggled to come up with an answer. I don't know why, but it always worked.

"Well," I said, and Sister smiled encouragingly. "We have these books that he left here. Traci wanted to return them to Duchat."

"Why, of course," she said. "Someone will be wanting Mr. Duchat's possessions. We ought to return these books right away."

Any of the Phillies could tell you that one of Sister Madonna's favorite maxims is "Procrastination is the thief of time." Consequently, I had no time for second thoughts before we arrived at Duchat's apartment.

"I hope we know what we're doing," I said as my Escort came to a stop in front of the building.

Sister Madonna patted my arm. "Go with the flow, Mrs. Galway," she advised. "Go with the flow."

"Sometimes the flow is headed for the rapids," I said. "Or a waterfall."

She laughed, and suddenly I felt more sanguine. I had to admit Madonna was turning out to be more fun than Ellen when it came to semi-legal activities.

I followed Sister Madonna to the door of the manager, where a granite-faced woman eyed us severely.

"Good afternoon," Sister Madonna said in her accustomed let's-get-down-to-business-and-get-this-taken-care-of voice. "We are from St. Philomena's School, and we wish to return a package that belonged to poor Mr. Duchat."

The manager peered at the package, then at Sister. She did not look at me, apparently regarding me as no more than a package-carrying flunky.

"I can't be responsible for Mr. Duchat's packages," she

said finally, her voice coming from her nose. "Not knowing when anyone will decide to get his belongings. All the things in his apartment, that's bad enough. What am I supposed to do with them, I ask you? Let alone take care of deliveries."

"Oh, certainly," Sister Madonna said. "We wouldn't dream of asking you to take care of this. It should be returned to his apartment, and that is our responsibility. If you would be so kind as to give us the key, we'll take care of it."

She looked doubtful. "I can't let anyone in the apartment. People are always coming around and wanting me to let them in. I tell them I can't do that."

"I quite understand," Sister said. "You are to be commended for your caution. Certainly you can't allow just anyone in."

"People don't understand," the woman said, sensing in Sister a kindred spirit of uprightness. "They don't see that I have a responsibility here, now that the poor man is dead."

"Of course you do," Sister agreed. "What reasons do these people have for wishing to enter Mr. Duchat's apartment, Mrs. . . . ?"

"Mrs. Zachariah," she said. "Oh, they all have their cock-and-bull stories, Sister. One of them said he delivered a package there by mistake and had to get it back."

"Imagine!" Sister murmured.

"Yes. Well, I saw through that. Then there was one woman who actually claimed to be Mrs. Duchat."

"Really!"

"Oh, there are always folks who want to poke around, you know. Any time some poor soul has a tragedy in his life, these vultures come around."

"My goodness," Sister said. "Well, we certainly would not want to disturb the poor man's home. But we do feel a real obligation to return his possessions. Surely he will have an heir to whom this will have meaning."

Mrs. Zachariah looked put-upon. "Well, I should hope so," she said. "I get no information from the police, you know. No one seems to understand that I need to clear that apartment out. We can't have apartments sitting vacant. And no rent coming in, of course. No one thinks about that.''

Sister Madonna made comforting sounds, and Mrs. Zachariah's face gradually cleared as she studied the serene countenance before her. While I waited, I meditated on the fine art of deceiving while telling the truth. My daughters had done this well during their long, long adolescence, but they had never developed such proficiency that I was unable to ferret out the real facts. Sister Madonna was good.

''Well, I guess I could let you in,'' Mrs. Zachariah said hesitantly. ''You understand, Sister, it isn't like I think you'd take anything. It's just, you know, if anyone was to know I'd let someone in, well . . .''

''Oh, please don't apologize, Mrs. Zachariah. You are absolutely right.''

Mrs. Z. hesitated for just another moment. ''I should go up with you,'' she said. ''But I was just about to leave for a doctor's appointment.''

''I quite understand,'' Sister said soothingly.

Seconds later we were in the elevator, key in hand, and in no time we were entering Mark Duchat's apartment.

''Quite a place,'' I said. Luxurious sofas flanked by marble-topped tables, an elaborate entertainment center, a well-stocked bar. Among the paintings I spotted a Matisse and a Renoir; given Duchat's proclivities, I wouldn't have wanted to vouch for their authenticity. Several large figurines posed on pedestals at one side of a bay window, and on the other side was an empty bookcase. The books were stacked on the floor, and papers and folders were piled on the tables as they had been left by the police investigators.

We zeroed in on the books. There weren't many—evidently Duchat had not been an avid reader. A number of art books, art histories, a few biographies, a set of Proust. And a volume of French poetry by Charles Baudelaire.

''*Fleurs du Mal,*'' I said, waving it at Sister before probing at the binding.

If we hadn't had a pretty good idea of what we were looking for, we would never have noticed the small overlap in the bottom of the lining inside the spine. As it was, it took a little coaxing with a letter opener before the key slid out—a small, flat key, like a suitcase key.

We sat and looked at it, basking in our cleverness for several minutes until it occurred to us that we had no idea what the key might unlock.

"A suitcase?" Sister suggested. "A briefcase, maybe?"

"I doubt it," I said. "Not if it's in the apartment. Whoever was searching wouldn't have worried about finding a key, he'd just break the latch on anything like that. Same with drawers or cabinets."

We considered a safety-deposit box, a locker at a health club, a trunk in a storage room in the apartment building. We discarded all of those ideas. The key wasn't like any of those, as far as either of us could recall.

We looked at each other gloomily for several minutes.

"Well," I said finally, "if you had information you were holding over someone's head, wouldn't you want to keep it where you could get at it quickly?"

"All right," Sister said. "Let's operate on that assumption for now. If there is a place in this apartment where such things can be kept, we ought to be able to find it. That's simple logic. Mr. Duchat was, after all, just a human being. What one human mind can conceive, another must be able to fathom."

It sounded good to me. We set about our fathoming.

For the next ten minutes, we looked behind paintings, probed the underside of furniture, lifted rugs. No keyhole showed itself.

"Well," I said, returning the cushion to the window seat I had just searched, "I hate to admit it, but Mr. Duchat has me stumped." I sat on the window seat and stared at the group of sculptures beside the window. They stared back.

Sister Madonna sat on the sofa and looked disappointed. "How can this be so difficult? Anything large enough to hold records of any importance ought to be visible, for heaven's sake. A drawer, a box, a cabinet. Why don't we see it?''

I scowled at a figurine of a three-headed dog that scowled back at me. Cerberus, the guard dog of Hades. *How appropriate,* I thought. Duchat's pet of choice.

I would have sworn the beast winked at me. ''Cerberus,'' I said, getting up and going slow-motion toward the statue. Sister Madonna raised her eyebrows at me.

The figurine was not as heavy as I had expected. I lifted it from its pedestal as Sister Madonna came across the room. Without asking, she helped me remove the marble top of the pedestal, and we stared at a small keyhole in the cube-shaped stand.

''There now!'' Sister Madonna clapped her hands. ''You see, you must never give up!''

It was the work of seconds to unlock the box. I reached inside and pulled out a small packet of letters, then a computer disk and a small box. A larger box, metal, was at the bottom.

We put our booty on the floor and checked it out. It took only a moment to see that the letters were from Omega Starlight. Tempting though it was, I refrained from reading them and turned my attention to the small box.

Inside was a silver identification bracelet with the initials S. C. and the date 6-17-84. A typed note in the same box read, *Remember? It's time for you to pay up. I just want what is mine.*

Sister Madonna and I looked at each other.

''Maybe the police will finally see a couple of other suspects now,'' I said.

''Excellent,'' she said. ''And what is in the other box?''

I opened it. It held money. Quite a bit of money. How much, I wasn't to discover, because we were interrupted at that point by a loud knock at the door.

''Police!'' said a firm voice. ''Open up.''

Chapter Twenty-two

"I don't believe this!" Adam said. It wasn't the first time he had said it. He clenched his fists against his temples in what I felt was a needlessly melodramatic gesture.

"Now she even has Sister Madonna doing it," Ellen said.

I took a sip of beer and eyed them coldly. "Well, if this is how you're going to be . . ."

"You are a nut case," Adam said, still cudgeling his head.

"Corrupting a nun is a mortal sin, Gen. What's next? Getting the Pope to be your wheel man?"

I sighed. "Sister Madonna wanted to do it. In fact, most of it was her idea."

"Oh, sure! Don't forget, Genevieve Lacy Galway, I happen to know of your persuasive tactics. You have no shame."

"An absolute nut case."

"I thought you'd be interested in what we found out," I said. "I had no idea you would be so fanatical about little technicalities. Well, my mistake."

Adam scowled mightily. "Concealing evidence is not a technicality. Obstructing justice is not a technicality. Lying to the police is not—"

"I beg your pardon! We did none of those things." Two snorts punctuated my defense. "Not exactly, anyway. We absolutely did not lie to the police. We simply didn't volunteer information. And we certainly have not obstructed

121

justice. We've been trying to promote justice, as a matter of fact.''

"You see?" Ellen said. "Soon she'll be canonizing herself."

I ignored her. "And as for concealing evidence, may I remind you that if it hadn't been for Madonna and me, the police wouldn't have found the letters or the bracelet? If you recall, they had searched Duchat's apartment before and hadn't thought to look inside the pedestals."

"How foolish of them," Ellen said.

As far as I was concerned, Sister Madonna and I weren't getting nearly the credit we deserved. Did the cops thank us for calling this cache of evidence to their attention? Oh, no, they were still too bothered about why we were there in the first place, though common sense would have suggested that if we hadn't been there, no one would have known there was evidence going to waste.

Of course, they pointed out that we had not called them, and that if Duchat's next-door neighbor had not heard sounds emanating from a supposedly vacant apartment, they would not have been there to share our discoveries. Naturally, Sister Madonna explained that we simply had not yet had time to notify them, since we had just that moment made our discoveries. They did not seem impressed.

Adam ground his teeth.

"But if you don't want to know what's on the computer disk, okay by me. Just forget I ever mentioned it." I helped myself to some popcorn and turned my attention to the Hideaway's television, where some animals appeared to be dining on some other animals.

"Oh, what the heck," Ellen grumbled. "So all right, what's on the disk?"

"Sure you want to know? I mean, I wouldn't want you to feel like an accessory or anything . . ."

"Tell already!"

"Okay. Records. Names, dates, amounts. Forged paintings sold by Victor Ingle—where they came from and who has them now. Sculpture smuggled by Clint Madison and sold to Ingle.''

''Oh ho!'' Ellen said.

''Yes. There were other people listed, too, people I never heard of. And descriptions of things sold at Cromwell Gallery—to whom, for how much. Doesn't say Sharon knew, but the implication would be enough to bring her down, I suppose. And there's information enough to make fools of a lot of well-known experts who authenticated the forgeries.''

''Anything about Traci?'' Adam asked.

I sighed. ''Mentions several paintings she sold to Ingle.''

''The records are what someone's looking for, I suppose,'' Ellen said. ''I don't see how it helps Traci, though.''

''True,'' I said. ''That was a disappointment. But it certainly does show that Traci wasn't the only one who had a reason to be angry at the man. And Traci wasn't the one searching for the evidence in her own apartment or in her classroom. Anyhow, there was other info on the disk.''

I took time to wet my whistle. Adam scowled. Ellen tapped her fingers.

I smiled at them. ''Well, there was a list of dates and amounts. No huge amounts, but substantial. No names, just initials.''

Adam rubbed his chin. ''Blackmail?''

''I don't know. I would have thought blackmail payments would be regular, you know—the same amounts, same initials. That's not what it looked like. It was more like a ledger, only without anything to show who paid for what. And every so often there was a total, with a number beside it, like a bank account number.''

''So maybe it's money he got from selling stolen items,'' Ellen said.

I nodded. ''That could explain the money in his hidey-hole. Then he deposits it in an account, probably under another name. I'm sure the police will be able to trace it.''

"Wait a minute," Adam said. "How do you know all this? Are you saying that after getting into Duchat's place under false pretenses, searching the place, scaring the neighbors—then the cops invited you down to check out the computer files?"

"Well," I said, "um. Not exactly." He waited. "Well, I just—um—see, I thought—actually, I didn't quite give them the disk." I waited for the explosion.

They didn't explode. They sat and stared at me for a long time. Finally Adam spoke, but in a much softer voice than I expected.

"You ran off with evidence? You just—helped yourself to a piece of evidence in a murder investigation?"

"No," I said. "Not exactly. It was an honest mistake. There was a lot of confusion. And then—well, I thought I might as well look at it, since I had it. After all, we found it. If I didn't look at it, how could I know if it was evidence or not? It might have been just more nasty art reviews."

"And now?" Adam asked in the same soft voice.

"Now I'm going to take it to the police," I said. "What else? I'm going there right now, in fact. I'll explain that in the confusion this afternoon, I overlooked it."

"Oh, can I come too?" Ellen asked. "I really want to see what happens when you pull that one. Also, I can probably arrange bail for you. If I want to, that is."

"Excuse me," Adam said. "Do I understand that you have this disk with you? You're carrying it around? A disk full of incriminating files that people have been searching for? One of whom may be a murderer? Is that what you're telling us?"

"Well, no one knows I have it," I pointed out reasonably. "Except for you two."

Adam looked at me in a rather unfriendly way. "I'll go with you," he said. "Nutty as you are, I'd hate to see you get killed. Sort of."

"Oh, very nice! Anyhow, it seems to me that both of

you are overlooking the most important thing we found. The ID bracelet.''

They looked at me without comprehension.

''Well, someone with the initials S. C. sent a note saying she just wants what is hers. Doesn't that sound threatening?''

''No,'' Ellen said.

''You're clutching at straws,'' Adam said.

''Fine. We'll just wait and see. Of course, we do have a suspect with those initials, but if that means nothing to you . . .''

Ellen nodded. ''Sharon Cromwell. Yes, I got that. All I'm saying is that it doesn't sound like a threat.''

''You have no imagination. Anyhow, I have to go now. Places to go, people to see. Someone mentioned going to a movie.''

''Oh, that,'' Adam said. ''I wasn't sure you had time in your busy schedule for non-criminal activities. By all means, let's go.''

''See if you can find a prison movie,'' Ellen said. ''It might give her something to think about.''

There was the matter of the disk to be seen to first. It could have been much more unpleasant, but, as Adam pointed out, the police were probably becoming inured. Frank Monroe squinched his eyes at me more than usual, and acted as if he didn't quite buy my story. I noticed that his young partner was beginning to look at me rather grimly as well, which shows how easily influenced some of us are by the company we keep. But after some unkind remarks and some forceful warnings, I was sent on my way.

It was late when we pulled up in front of my building. A red MG pulled out just in time to present us with a parking place, and I invited Adam up for coffee.

''Cream or sugar?'' I asked. ''Or skim milk and artificial sweetener?''

"Black," Adam said. "You got a paper towel? Your vase fell over."

"Here." I handed him a couple of towels. "What vase?"

"On the desk. Water made a puddle."

I poured the coffee and carried the mugs into the living room where Adam was mopping up the spill from my over-turned bud vase.

"I think you're going to have a stain on the wood," he said. "Water's been sitting there for a little while."

A prickle ran across my shoulders.

"How?" I said. "What?"

He looked at me quizzically. "Care to elaborate?"

I found a few more words. "How did it get knocked over? I thought you meant you knocked it over. If it's been upset for a while, if I didn't do it this morning, if it isn't dried by now . . ." This was beginning to sound like a lit-any. I knew what I meant, but it wasn't coming out right.

However, Adam seemed to get the drift. He looked at the three doors opening off the living room—two bed-rooms, one bath.

"Get out," he said quietly. "If you hear anything, run like the dickens and call 911."

"But, Adam, you—"

"Go!"

I went. I cowered in the hall for several years, until he finally emerged.

"No one's here," he said. "Let's look around."

I checked out the desk drawers, then all the other drawers I could think of. By the time I had finished, my heart was no longer hammering.

"I don't know," I said. "Everything's there. But it looks—different. Maybe just because I know someone was here."

"There's no sign that the door was forced," Adam said.

I sighed. "I wish I had a cat to blame it on." Then I remembered my missing keys. I had a spare set, of course, and considering the other things that had been competing for my attention, lost keys hadn't seemed so important. In retrospect, I could see how that might not have been a really wise attitude.

"Someone stole your keys? When? Why didn't you get your lock changed?" he asked, frowning ferociously.

"Well, Adam, I didn't have time yet. It only happened yesterday."

"And of course you were very busy today. Unfortunately, criminals seldom take weekends off if they have work to do. They are very dedicated to their careers."

I ignored the sarcasm. "Why would anyone be looking for something here?"

"Maybe someone saw you and your crony going into Duchat's place. Maybe he thought it was worth a shot to see if you found what he was looking for."

"Maybe *she* thought," I said. "Remember the ID bracelet?"

"I don't really care, he, she, so what? Someone is watching you, Gen, and . . ."

"Well, now he—or she—knows I don't have anything here. So he won't bother me again."

From the look on Adam's face, I judged that he wasn't buying my nonchalant act. Well, why should he? I was having a hard enough time convincing myself.

Chapter Twenty-three

I was not a happy woman. The police had come to my apartment on Saturday night to join Adam in a blame-the-victim orgy. Everyone seemed to enjoy lecturing about the perils of disregarding good advice, poking one's nose into things that were guaranteed to get one in trouble, and not having one's locks changed when one's keys disappeared.

After the cops were through browbeating me, Adam took over and insisted on taking me to his place for the night. Not for any delightful interlude, I assure you, since, even if I had had any romantic inclinations heretofore, they would have been curdled by then. It was clear that my other choice would be to have him spend the night sleeping on my doorstep, and I was not prepared to awaken speculations in Mrs. Shelby's mind.

Adam, in his role of martyr, insisted on giving up his bedroom and folding his large frame into the sofa. It served him right, as far as I was concerned.

And, of course, I had not brought along my Sunday-go-to-meeting clothes, which necessitated a detour to my place before Mass, and led to my entry just behind Father Tim. A fact that was not lost on the Phillies who happened to be at the ten o'clock Mass.

I threw myself on Ellen's mercy after Mass, since I was sure Adam would never allow me to stay alone, and I was none too thrilled at the prospect of being scowled at by him for another night. Fortunately, Ellen was glad to offer me a bed for the night. Well, why not? It gave her a chance to exercise her own I-told-you-sos.

But all of that I could rise above. I have, after all, been yelled at for many years by many people, and it's never stopped me yet.

What really teed me off was the idea that someone had entered my apartment uninvited, had pawed through my letters and bills and receipts and notices that I might have won the Publishers Clearing House sweepstakes. Never mind that I had nothing to hide, that no one would ever be able to blackmail me with the detritus of my sedate life. It was the principle, the affront. How dare he (or she) snoop around in my private life? Adam had suggested that I had a lot of room to talk, considering that I had been doing the very same thing. And that was why I was not terribly fond of Adam at the moment.

Anyhow, we now had another prime suspect, as far as I was concerned. Even Sgt. Monroe showed a flicker of interest in the ID bracelet, as well as in Omega's letters.

"But, Geneviève, I can not believe Sharon has killed someone," Traci said. "She is a very nice person."

We were gathered in Ellen's living room for brunch after Mass—Ellen, Donald, Traci, and I—to brainstorm about the discoveries Sister Madonna and I had made. Donald had been dropped from my list of suspects, at least for the time being. He certainly hadn't harmed Traci, and it seemed unlikely that he had been stalking me at St. Phil's the same night Traci had sent him to her apartment. He had left his car parked at the gym, he said, hoping to be unnoticed if he approached Traci's on foot.

"And the note doesn't sound like anything Sharon would write," Ellen added. "Why would she write 'Remember me?' She saw Duchat pretty often."

"But we don't know when the note was written," I said. "Maybe it was when he first turned up here."

"Which was three or four years ago," Donald said. "So why would she wait till now to kill him?"

"Maybe she just gave up on getting what she wanted,"

I said, scowling at him. This was not going as I had planned.

"Anyhow," Traci said, "there may be someone else that we do not know that possesses those initials S. C."

I sighed. "I don't want it to be someone we don't know! Because then how will we ever find her?"

"My goodness," Ellen said, "maybe we'll have to let the police find her. I know that's a radical idea, but . . ."

"Also," I said, flapping a hand at her, "there are those letters. So Omega is a good suspect, too."

"This is hard," Ellen said. "You see, this is probably why people go to school to learn how to solve crimes, instead of just taking it up as a mid-life hobby."

"You may be right," I said. "And speaking of school, many long years ago, when I was just a simple English teacher, I had some papers to grade. I think I'd better go home and get them and start earning my salary. I'll be back shortly."

Donald and Traci insisted on following me to my apartment.

"You cannot be too careful, Geneviève," Traci said. "If this person is still trying to find something, he may return to your home. Who knows if he may hurt you?"

"Unlikely," I said. I had a feeling that I was now to be typecast as the fragile, helpless little victim, a role I had never much enjoyed. A person who stops growing at five foot one is in danger of such misperceptions at every turn. But Traci looked so anxious that I gave in, though with poor grace.

Spring was in the air again and the streets were busy with college students heading for the park beyond the row of tidy brick apartment buildings. I maneuvered around bikes and jaywalkers until the street turned modern and elegant, the neighborhood where Mark Duchat had lived. No college students here, nor schoolteachers, either.

Without the distractions, my mind started poking around again at the ID bracelet. If S. C. was Sharon, would she and Duchat start a business relationship? Unless he was paying her in installments; he did owe her money. But then why would she kill him?

Of course, there was the possibility that S. C. had changed her name. That would explain why she sent the bracelet with the note, to identify herself to him. I liked that idea better. Except that if S. C. killed Duchat, she had to be someone who was at the gallery that night.

I sighed in frustration. Ellen was right, this was hard. My brain cells spun idly while I drove through the downtown area, mostly deserted today, and finally tossed out one more speculation: There was one person who had changed her name. Omega Starlight. At least that was what Duchat had implied in his review of her work, and it certainly seemed like an invented name. And she was at the gallery.

I reached my own quiet neighborhood and turned at my street just as I shot down my last inspiration. Why in the world would Omega have gotten involved in an affair with Duchat if he had cheated her in some way?

I gave up, pulled into the parking lot, and stomped grumpily into the house, followed by Traci and Donald.

There was no sign that anyone had been there since I had left. The answering machine light was on, and I ran the tape while I gathered my schoolwork.

"Hi, Mom." Annie's voice. "What's going on there? I hope you're just out having a good time and neglecting your duties. I'm going to Connecticut today—this is Sunday, incidentally—so I'll call again when I get back Tuesday night. I have some info."

I felt a rush of relief; at least Annie was safe.

A message from Polly Fresno told me about a Victorian music box she had just gotten at her shop. One from Marty Quinn reminded me that our thirty-fifth high school reunion was in June and I absolutely had to come. One from Nora asked if "my" murder had been solved yet.

The tape issued a couple of clicks, and then a voice,

whispering: "Quit snooping into things that aren't your business. Next time you may not get away free."

The three of us sat and stared at the machine for a while in the ensuing silence.

"Oh, *mon Dieu*," Traci said at last. "You see, you are in danger, Geneviève."

Donald cleared his throat. "Well, we'll have to take this to the police, Gen. Maybe they can find out whose voice is on the tape. Or is it just in the movies where they can do that kind of thing?"

I didn't know. I supposed I would have to take the tape to the police, a prospect I relished as much as eating worms. It gave me another reason to resent the intruder.

And if he imagined that this was the way to make me back off, it was clear that he did not know me at all.

Chapter Twenty-four

When I stopped in the faculty lounge on Monday morning, Mr. Merryman was lying in wait for me.

"I got your keys here, Miz Galway." He shook them in front of me to prove it, but he wasn't ready to give them to me yet, of course.

"Oh, that's wonderful," I said, willing myself not to flush with guilt. "I . . ."

"Found 'em in the hall by 103," he said, scowling at me.

"Yes," I said. "I dropped them—you know, there was an intruder on Friday night, and . . ."

He brushed that aside. I would not get off by blaming my irresponsibility on stray intruders. "You teachers got to be more careful with the keys. Can't be too careful with them young devils around. Never know what they'll get into."

"Oh, I know," I said. "I really didn't . . ."

"Now if one of them would have found them keys and got into something, then what? What would Sister say about that?"

"Well, I . . ."

"You take better care now, Miz Galway. All you teachers got to take these things more serious." Finally he handed over the keys and stumped away.

"Well, Gen, I hope you're satisfied," Ellen said. "You got all us teachers in trouble."

"How shocking," Bernadette said. "Tossing your keys around willy-nilly. How irresponsible."

"You're lucky the merry man didn't revoke your key privileges entirely," Ellen said.

"Oh, do not tease Geneviève," Traci said. "Here, I have made the coffee today. This is coffee Sharon Cromwell has given me. Is it not delicious?"

We accepted the offer and approved the brew.

"It *is* good," Bernadette said. "What kind is it?"

"Almond mocha, I think," Traci said. "Sharon has always different kinds. She is, you know, a—an addict!"

I sipped morosely. "Now, how could those keys have been by Traci's classroom? I looked all around there when the police were here on Friday night. They weren't there."

"The drinking fountain is right there, isn't it?" Sarah asked. "Maybe the keys got pushed into the corner by the fountain."

"Maybe," I said, unconvinced.

"It doesn't seem likely the intruder would have taken the keys and then brought them back," Bernadette said. "Why would he do that?"

"Maybe he didn't want me to know he'd been in my apartment," I said.

Bernadette dropped her spoon and Sarah knocked over the tea canister.

"Someone broke into your place, too?" Sarah asked.

I nodded. "He was a lot neater in his operation there than at Traci's or Duchat's. I probably wouldn't have known anyone was there if he hadn't knocked over a vase. After I got to looking around, it seemed as if papers and books had been moved around. Just like Traci's intruder, he didn't take anything. Obviously just searching."

Bernadette shivered. "Well, I wish he'd find whatever it is, so he'd let people alone."

"Amen," Ellen said. "Gen, you did call about getting your lock changed, I hope?"

"First thing this morning," I said. "The super will take care of it. Not that I think it matters. By now whoever he is, he knows I don't have anything he wants. The police have it all.''

Everyone in Derry knew all about it, in fact, thanks to the industrious reporters, who had already found out about our discoveries. Traci had been replaced, at least temporarily, as a media star, by Sharon Cromwell and Omega Starlight. The fact that no one knew the contents of Omega's letters didn't stop the more flamboyant reporters from hinting at sordid secrets. The ID bracelet seemed to be of much greater interest to the newsfolk than it had been to Adam and Ellen, and they didn't hesitate to point out that Sharon possessed the appropriate initials.

Unfortunately, Sister Madonna and I were prominently mentioned on the news, as well, which did not give us much hope that the Phillies would settle down and forget the recent events.

The first bell rang and we went forth to our daily battle against the forces of darkness. There was still something about the keys that bothered me, something nagging at the edges of my mind, that wouldn't quite speak up. I finally assigned it to my subconscious. Sooner or later it would surface.

Meanwhile I struggled to drag my various charges through *The Mill on the Floss*, Lady Macbeth's hand-washing problems, ''The Ransom of Red Chief,'' and the woes of the ancient mariner. It was no mean task, considering that the Phillies were united in their determination to discuss the events that had brought Sister Madonna and me to the front page of the Sunday *Sentinel*.

Sister Madonna sent an office Phillie to ask me to stop by the office at lunchtime, and I found my coconspirator looking a shade less serene than usual.

''Oh, Mrs. Galway,'' she said, ''I just wanted to warn you that we are surrounded by reporters. They have been in my office this morning, wanting to know about our little—adventure.''

"What could they possibly want to ask us?" I wondered. "They seem to have all the information already."

She sighed. "Heaven knows. But I'm sure they'll be waiting for you after school. They wanted to come up to your classroom, if you can believe that! During the school day!"

"The girls would have loved it," I said.

"Undoubtedly. And we have quite enough trouble on that score." She sighed and pressed her fingertips to her forehead.

"Trouble?"

"Some of the parents are toying with the idea of transferring their daughters. Well, you can hardly blame them. They're worried about the girls' safety. It was bad enough that a murder occurred in the gallery where they were all milling about. Then when suspicion fell on one of our teachers . . ."

"I'm sure I'd have been a little worried as a parent, too," I said.

"Then that was just dying down when we had the intruder, followed by Mr. Tomcyk's arrest. And now you and I show up in the news!"

"But Sister," I protested, "we were in there as the good guys! Just innocent bystanders who found some helpful evidence."

"Yes," she said, with just a trace of irony in her tone. "But it's just one more thing to remind them that their daughters' school is associated with a murder. It isn't the kind of atmosphere to build parental confidence."

I promised to avoid the reporters and went to eat my politically correct lunch, which certainly contained nothing to take my mind off the current woes.

"Hello?" Ellen said, nudging me.

"What?"

"I've been talking to you for five minutes," she said.

Traci laughed. "I think she is gathering wool."

"And that's all I'm gathering," I said. "I had hoped to

capture some half-gelled idea about keys, but no such luck.''

''What about keys?'' Ellen asked.

I frowned at her. ''Weren't you listening? I don't know what about them. It just seems as if I ought to know something.''

''Don't think about it,'' Ellen said. ''The more you try, the less you'll remember. If you ignore it, it'll pop up sooner or later.''

''That's my plan,'' I said. ''Now, my next problem is how to avoid the reporters waiting for me after school.''

''Tell them you've promised an exclusive to the *Beacon*,'' Ellen suggested. ''Which you must, by the way. Our crack team of investigative journalists is even now working on the case. They will be interviewing you, I promise.''

''A prospect I look forward to, I'm sure. However, I doubt that will scare away the newspersons lurking outside.''

''Leave through the gym,'' Bernadette said. ''You can come out with me.''

The sophomore Phillies were clustered at the windows when I got to the classroom, and the chorus of squeals, giggles, and moans suggested that one of the more popular rock groups might be setting up on the soccer field.

But no. It was merely Mr. Tomcyk, wearing shorts as he led the freshmen (lucky ducks!) in his afternoon gym class. One of the cruelties inflicted by the tyrants who ran St. Phil's was to assign the sophomore gym class to Mrs. Melendez. Sister Madonna was no dummy.

''Perhaps we might take our seats now,'' I suggested, not being any less cruel than the other tyrants. ''Today we can consider the romantic implications of 'The Lost Phoebe.' ''

Reluctantly they peeled their eyes from the legs of Mr. Tomcyk and drooped back to their seats.

''Who are those people watching from behind the fence?'' Bridget asked.

"Baseball scouts, I imagine," I said. I supposed they were the reporters, killing time until they were permitted to pounce on some of us.

Not much gets past the Phillies, unfortunately.

"They're reporters," Denny said. "I talked to some of them at lunchtime. They asked me about you, Mrs. Galway." The cobalt eyes sparkled at me.

"Ah, well," I said. "The burdens of fame. Now . . ."

"You didn't tell us about the robber, Mrs. Galway." Jean Ann fixed me with a reproachful look.

"When we saw you crawling around in the bushes," Bridget said, "why didn't you tell us the robber was chasing you?"

"Maybe we could have caught him," Kim added.

I sighed. "That's exactly why I didn't tell you. All we need is to have you girls playing cops and robbers. Amateurs should leave crime fighting to the police." I had the grace to blush, but luckily the girls didn't know why.

"Anyway," Bridget said, "we could have told the cops who was around here, given a description, I mean. If we'd known there was a crook, we'd have paid more attention."

"Wait a minute," I said. "You can still tell about anyone you saw. You mean you did see someone around the school?"

"Well, yes," Denny said. "A couple of people. But we didn't pay much attention, like I said. Because we didn't know anything was wrong." She eyed me accusingly.

"So we couldn't give a good description," Jean Ann said sorrowfully.

I gritted my teeth, Theodore Dreiser forgotten. "Girls, whatever you saw might help. Someone was near the school? When? Where?"

A babble arose, and finally Bridget got the floor. "Well, after we saw you in the bushes, Mrs. Galway. Because before then we were at choir practice, you know. And then we saw you. And then we walked by the convent with you. And then we walked back by the school because Denny was supposed to mail some bills for her mother, only she forgot, so we went back to where the mailbox is.''

I scowled at her. "Are we getting somewhere close to seeing someone?"

"That was when. There was a lady walking her dog. She had gray hair, I remember, and the dog was—"

"I think we can rule her out," I said. "I believe I would have noticed a dog."

"Okay. Then there was a dude riding a bicycle; he was wearing dark jeans and a—sweatshirt, I think. Dark. And there was another guy who was older, and he limped, like he had a bad leg. He was fat. And he had a little white beard."

"There was a woman who came down the street beside the school, too," Denny said. "She was wearing dark slacks and a jacket. At least I think it was a woman. She had long blond hair. But I couldn't see her face because she was going the other way. But she walked like a woman. I think."

Among my suspects there were no fat men with white beards, no gray-haired ladies, with or without dogs. Sharon was a blonde, and I supposed she didn't have to wear her hair in a twist all the time. Omega Starlight was a brunette, but she was no stranger to the wig concept.

"Do you remember anything more about the man on the bicycle?" I asked. "Anything at all?"

Five foreheads crinkled, five pairs of eyes squinted, as the rest of the class watched the thought process at work.

"He was a little bit old," Jean Ann ventured. "His face was kind of, you know, with lines?"

"A little bit old?"

"Like thirty-five or something," Peggy said. "And he had dark hair. I think."

"Yes," Kim said. "Real dark. And he had a ponytail, because when he looked down the street it flip-flopped."

After gazing at one another for a few moments, they all nodded.

"That's all, Mrs. Galway," Bridget said. "Like I said, we didn't really think about noticing anything in particular."

"And there was Mr. Tomcyk," Kim said, and heads swiveled toward her. "We saw him there, too, remember?"

Exclamations pelted her from all sides.

"Well, duh!" Bridget said. "We're talking about strangers. What does Mr. Tomcyk have to do with it?"

"Mr. Tomcyk certainly isn't a murderer!" Denny snapped.

"I was just saying," Kim said, shrinking.

After another round of glares, the Phillies returned their attention to me.

"Do you think that helps?" Peggy asked.

"It might," I said, my voice sounding tinny in my ears. My mind was helpfully replaying for me the sight of Clint Madison advancing toward me, chain in hand, ponytail flicking as he spun around.

"Well," I said, "I guess that's enough detecting for today. In the interest of being called a literature class, do let us devote some time to poor Phoebe."

Chapter Twenty-five

By Tuesday morning I still hadn't decided whether to tell the police about the possible identity of the St. Phil prowler. It was admittedly slim evidence, and, given that the cops were none too fond of me at the moment, I thought they might be disinclined to listen to my theories. I also hadn't figured out what was bothering me about the keys. I had, however, succeeded in keeping myself awake half the night with those thoughts as well as worries about Annie, so Tuesday was not one of my better ones.

A flock of reporters still lurked near the school. I had avoided them in the morning by concealing myself among a crowd of Phillies, but I noticed they were still there at last period. Sarah, coming back from an errand, was almost waylaid, but ducked between the bushes and came around the tennis court.

"Leave with us," Donald suggested. "Through the gym."

"That is a good idea, Donald," Traci said. "Geneviève can come with us to the gallery, and then we will come back and get her car. The reporters will by then be gone, *n'est-ce pas?*"

"Why are you going to the gallery?" Ellen scowled suspiciously.

Traci laughed. "We are not playing the detectives, Ellen. Sharon has said I may come and get my paintings, the ones Mark was selling."

It sounded like a good idea. Besides avoiding the press,

it might allow an opportunity to chat with Sharon about the bracelet. I decided not to mention that to Ellen.

On the way to the gallery I told Traci and Donald about the girls' information. I still wasn't sure I should tell the police; after all, I had seen Donald there, too. Clint Madison, if in fact that was who the girls had seen, could have been just another innocent passerby.

Donald was adamant, however. "The cops aren't going to hang him just because he was riding past the school. But it wouldn't hurt to check him out."

Traci agreed. "Clint does have a great temper, Geneviève. I do not think he is a bad person, but he could maybe strike in anger before he thinks. And if one has killed, one would wish to find anything that would make the police suspect it."

We agreed that we'd stop at the station and tattle on Clint after picking up Traci's painting. Donald parked his Saturn in front of the entrance, behind a red MG.

A shiver ran down my spine, a phenomenon with which I was becoming annoyingly familiar. It suddenly seemed to me that I was seeing an alarming number of red MGs all of a sudden. At Victor Ingle's office building. At Omega's show downtown. In front of my house. The symptom was not eased by the sight of Victor Ingle, leaning against the MG, in a spirited debate with Omega Starlight.

They looked up as we approached, and their attitude was far from welcoming.

"Traci." Ingle nodded at her, but his black agate eyes were for me alone. "Well, Mrs. Galway. We do seem to keep meeting, don't we?"

"Actually, we just missed meeting on Saturday night, didn't we?" I asked, noticing that I hadn't yet learned to keep my mouth shut.

He raised a quizzical eyebrow. "Saturday night? Could I have failed to notice you, Mrs. Galway? It hardly seems likely."

"Probably you didn't see me," I said. "You were just

driving away when I arrived home. I did wonder why you had come to call on me.''

''I beg your pardon?'' He looked completely astounded. ''Why ever would I call on you, Mrs. Galway? You'll forgive me, but we have not established what I would call a cordial relationship.''

''Perhaps it wasn't me, but my apartment that you wanted to visit,'' I said, wondering if he could really be that talented an actor. Could the glut of red MGs be a coincidence?

He smiled thinly. ''Perhaps your feverish activities of late have unhinged you, my good woman. I assure you that I would not at all wish to visit your apartment, if I even knew where it might be.''

Omega Starlight, who today was wearing her dark tresses in a braided crown, giving her an imposing presence, chimed in at that point. ''Mrs. Galway seems to have an insatiable desire to cause trouble for everyone who crosses her path. I understand that I have you to thank for making my private correspondence a matter for police scrutiny.''

''Oh, Omega, that is not just,'' Traci said. ''Geneviève has done only what she must when she finds something that is to do with a crime.''

''I had nothing to do with any crime!'' Omega glared at her. ''You, my dear, on the other hand . . .''

''That's enough!'' Donald gave a glare of his own. ''Traci didn't kill anyone!''

Omega shrugged. ''Perhaps. I was not referring to the demise of Mark Duchat, which I regard as more of a public service than a crime. Dear Traci is guilty of the much more serious offense of forgery.''

''I did not . . . !'' Traci cried out.

''Never mind,'' Donald said. ''Let's go and get your paintings.''

Cloaked in silence, the five of us stalked into the gallery. The guard seated at the door eyed us incuriously. A couple of women were browsing, and a student sat sketching a landscape.

"Sharon must be in her office," Traci said. "I will tell her I have come for the painting."

We followed her down the hallway, Ingle and Omega trailing after us. Traci tapped at the office door. There was no response, but behind the door we heard a voice: *"Buenos días, Señora. ¿Quiere usted decirme dónde está el mercado?"* ("Good morning, señora. Can you tell me where the market is?")

"Ah," Traci said, "Sharon is practicing her Spanish lesson. She has been planning a trip to Spain in the fall, and she has acquired these language tapes."

She tapped again and opened the door. "Sharon? I am sorry to disturb, but . . . Sharon, what is wrong?"

She took a step into the office and I peered around her. Sharon Cromwell was seated at her desk, her head cradled in her arms. She didn't respond.

"Sharon?" Traci repeated. "What is it?" She moved toward the desk, and the rest of us followed.

"Por favor, Señor, ¿puede usted ayudarme?" the tape asked placidly. *"Necesito un médico.* ("Please, sir, can you help me? I need a doctor.")

Donald strode to the desk and leaned over Sharon. Then he dashed around the desk and put his hand against Sharon's neck. He looked shell-shocked.

"Call 911," he said, his voice strained. "I think she's dead."

"Oh, no!" Traci gasped. "Oh, *mon Dieu!*"

Behind me, Omega chittered like a monkey. I grabbed a tissue from my purse and used it to lift the phone receiver and punch 911. Victor Ingle leaned against the door frame and held his handkerchief over his mouth.

"¿Dónde está el cuarto de baño?" the tape inquired. ("Where is the bathroom?")

I recited the necessary information to the dispatcher and hung up. We all stood mute and shivering, our eyes darting about, trying to look at something other than the still form at the desk. The clear calm voice on the tape sought directions to a restaurant and ordered a dinner. In the background something hummed steadily, and for want of anything better to do, my brain traced the noise to the air conditioner. That explained not only the humming but the shivering, I realized. It was cold in the office, and I wondered why Sharon would have turned the machine up that high on a chilly spring day.

I also realized that there was another humming sound, which I finally traced to the computer sitting patiently waiting for instructions, a page of text displayed.

Grateful for something to look at other than poor Sharon Cromwell, I scanned the text, a letter outlining plans for a show to be held at the gallery. I glanced at the printer and found the letter printed out. I had just started to read it when Donald said, ''She left a note.''

''A letter,'' I said. ''I was just reading it.''

He shook his head. ''No, I mean a note, here, on the desk.'' He pointed to a sheet of paper beside Sharon's arm.

It was neatly typed, brief, and to the point: *I am truly sorry. It was an accident. I just can't stand any more. S. C.*

''Suicide?'' Omega asked, sounding relieved. I looked at her. ''Well, it's just . . . I thought—well, after Mark . . .''

Beside the note were a coffee mug and a pill bottle, both empty.

''Oh, no,'' Traci said. ''Why would she do so?''

''Maybe she figured it was only a matter of time before the police found enough evidence to charge her,'' Donald said. ''After she knew they found the ID bracelet . . .''

''Pretty extreme, isn't it?'' I asked. ''If she killed Duchat accidentally, the penalty surely wouldn't have been as severe as suicide.''

''Look, shouldn't we be waiting outside?'' Victor asked. He still looked ashen. ''Do we have to stay in here with—with the . . .''

''I don't see why we can't wait in the hallway,'' I said.

"It isn't like we have to guard anything. No one can come in without our seeing him."

Having given ourselves permission, we moved out with alacrity and stood in the hallway. Within ten minutes the representatives of law and medicine began arriving to do their various things. Much to my chagrin, Sgt. Monroe was among them; surely the man was terribly overworked.

Right away I could see that I was not alone in chagrin-dom, as Frank's eyes located me.

"I wish I could say I'm surprised to see you here, Gen," he said. I wasn't sure whether he was smiling or merely baring his teeth at me. "Is this a new hobby you've taken up?"

"No one is more reluctant than I to keep running into you this way, Sergeant," I said with great dignity. "I am certainly not involved in this situation at all. I am merely an innocent bystander."

"Yes," he said, moving into the doorway. "What's that darn racket?"

"It's a tape recorder," I said. "It was on when we got here. We left it on because we thought we shouldn't touch anything," I added virtuously.

"Well, that's a welcome addition to your repertoire," he said, and went about his business, after telling us all to hang around for a while.

Victor slumped in a chair near the doorway, casting an occasional irritated glance at Omega, who paced back and forth across the gallery. Traci and Donald sat on a bench at the far side of the room, looking depressed.

There was something about the scene in Sharon's office that bothered me, but I didn't know what it was. I reminded myself that, as so many people had told me recently, I was not a detective, ergo it was not my job to worry about such things. Unfortunately, I don't listen to my own advice any more than to anyone else's, so I kept worrying about it as I drifted around the gallery staring at whatever happened to be hanging on the walls.

Still stewing, I wandered down the hallway, past the rest rooms, past Sharon's office, toward the studio. Just as I reached the studio, the door flew open, and Clint Madison erupted, carrying a mallet.

My scream brought as much reaction as any damsel in distress could possibly hope for. Cops boiled out of the office. From the main gallery ran Traci and Donald, Omega and Victor, the innocent art lovers, and the guard. Clint stood before me, wide-eyed and wide-mouthed. Questions were shouted at me.

"He—he," I squeaked, pointing at Clint. "He . . ."

It was humiliating. I had always imagined myself the kind of woman who would remain cool and calm in such circumstances. I was, after all, regularly visited by calamities, being both a mother and a teacher. Yet here I stood, bleating like a sheep.

"What?" Clint sounded outraged. "What did I do to you? Are you nuts or what?"

I caught my breath. "It was—I just—you scared me."

He glared at me. "I scared you? Try opening your door and having a crazy woman screech in your face sometime! Why would you be scared of me?"

I thought it would be a breach of etiquette to mention his undeniably fearsome appearance. "I wasn't expecting the door to open," I said lamely. "I didn't know anyone was in there."

He continued to glower. "It's a studio. I work there sometimes. On the other hand, I sure don't know why you're here." For the first time he took notice of the uniforms surrounding us. "What's going on?"

"Did you see Sharon today?" I asked, relieved to note that I was regaining my customary nosiness. Frank Monroe huffed an exasperated breath in my ear.

Clint shook his head. "Her door was locked. I figured she was gone to lunch."

"What time was that?" I asked.

"I don't know, one o'clock, one-thirty maybe. Why? Did something happen to her?"

"Mrs. Galway, may I speak to you for a minute?" Frank said. "If you can take just a little break from your investigating duties, that is."

"Tell him about Friday night," Donald said.

"What about Friday night?" Frank and I chorused.

"At school. You know."

"Oh," I said. "Well, I don't know if it means anything."

Frank stared at me semi-patiently. I told him about the sighting of someone who might have been Clint Madison near St. Phil's, keeping a nervous eye on the proposed villain as I did so. Frank didn't seem impressed, and even to me it sounded less than awesome.

Clint, however, did seem impressed, or, more accurately, infuriated. "What the devil business is it of yours where I go?" he thundered. "I can't ride on a public street without yours say-so? What is it with you, lady?"

"So you were riding there on Friday?" I asked. It wasn't exactly what he had said, but it was close enough.

He squinched his eyes at me. "More than likely. Not that it's any of your business, but I live on Towson Street, two blocks past the school. It's the route I usually take home from my studio. I didn't know I needed permission."

"Mrs. Galway is a little confused," Frank said. "Ever since she got this delusion that she's a detective." He took my arm and rather firmly led me to an unoccupied bit of hallway where he delivered a lecture that ended with a suggestion that I might be spending time in the pokey if I chose to disregard his advice.

"Now," he concluded, "I have to take statements from the other people who were here. I do this sort of thing alone. Understand?"

I nodded. "My lips are sealed. But Frank . . ."

He pointed a stern index finger at me.

"I know, I know. But, Frank, there's something wrong

about that scene in the office. I don't know what, but there's something.''

He smiled. ''Maybe we'll find it, then. Sometimes we do, you know. Otherwise, folks would stop paying us.''

Sighing, I followed him and stood obediently silent while he took information from the others.

The student and the art lovers meekly identified themselves, explained their presence, and disavowed any and all knowledge of any untoward happenings. The guard, who was properly shocked, explained that people came and went during the day without any interference from him, unless they should happen to be carrying a painting or sculpture tucked under their coats.

Neither Victor nor Omega were the least bit amenable to being questioned.

''I do not understand what business it is of the authorities where I go or why,'' Omega declared, staring frostily at this minion of the law. ''What possible bearing can my activities have on this poor woman's suicide?''

''Ms. Cromwell's death hasn't been ruled a suicide yet,'' Frank said mildly. ''Until it is—''

''Wait a minute!'' Victor Ingle yelped. ''What does that mean? You think it isn't a suicide?''

Frank shook his head. ''What I think doesn't matter, sir. The coroner will decide the cause of death. Until then, I have my own job to do. And my job, right now, is to find out what you were doing here.''

Ingle harrumphed and rolled his eyes. ''This is an art gallery, Sergeant. I am an art dealer. Simple, is it not?''

''You had business here today?'' Frank was unflappable.

''I had a painting to pick up for a client of mine.''

''Ms. Cromwell was expecting you?''

''Of course she was expecting me. I called her this morning, at about eleven.''

''And there was no indication that Ms. Cromwell was despondent?''

Victor deflated. "No. No, she sounded perfectly—I never suspected she . . ."

Frank nodded and turned his attention to Omega Starlight, who, after an elaborate paragraph of body language expressing her extreme displeasure, deigned to answer some questions. She had come to discuss with Sharon some drawings to be included in the show she was planning for August.

"I had dropped off some things over the weekend," she said. "I called Sharon today at a little after one. And nothing seemed wrong. I spoke to her for only a moment, of course. She said she was with a client. And she asked me to come in this afternoon."

"No idea who the client might have been?" Frank asked, and received a shake of the head in answer.

Traci explained our presence. Sharon had left a message at school for her, saying she could come by and pick up her paintings.

"Funny you should all have arrived at the same time," Frank said, observing us to note any sign that we found it funny as well.

"Well, we don't know that we did," I said, and five pairs of eyes fastened on me, two pairs puzzled, two irritated, and one unreadable. "Well, I only meant, to be strictly accurate, Traci, Donald, and I arrived together. We don't know when Ms. Starlight and Mr. Ingle arrived, or if they were together. For all we know, one of them—or both—could have been leaving when we got here."

"What are you trying to say?" Omega's eyes tried hard to set me ablaze. "Why would I have come back inside if I were leaving when you got here?"

Ingle's lips curved into an unamused smile. "She's suggesting that, in the event Sharon's death was not a suicide, you may have wished to be in on the discovery, in the company of others."

"I?" Her voice rose to a shriek. "Perhaps she was suggesting that of you, my dear Victor! And she may be right.

You were at the entrance when I arrived, after all. And everyone knew that you and Sharon—''

''Shut your mouth, you stupid ninny! You know darn well I just got here. You were coming around the side of the building. Where had *you* been, by the way?''

Frank sighed wearily. ''Everyone's an interrogator, I see. Well, I need the practice anyhow, so maybe you'll just humor me. Now you two,'' he said, indicating Omega and Victor, ''I'd like to talk to both of you for just a few more minutes. The rest of you can go on home for now, and try to stay out of trouble.''

We agreed to try, and left quickly, carrying scars from Victor's and Omega's eyes in our backs.

Chapter Twenty-six

"I just didn't believe it would turn out to be Sharon Cromwell," Ellen said. "I was rooting for Ingle."

"I am so surprised also," Traci said. "And sad that she would kill herself. Mark, he was not worth so much sorrow. I am sorry to say so, since he is dead, but it is true."

I took another slice of pizza. "Did you hear anything yet, Adam?"

"Like what?"

"Anything," I said. "From your friends with badges. About Sharon."

"I haven't talked to anyone," Adam said, looking at me curiously. "What did you think I might hear?"

"Gen thinks it might not be suicide," Donald said.

Ellen sighed. "I might have known. Tell us, Sherlock, what did you discover that the dim-witted police missed?"

"I'd think, since you're lounging around my apartment, you might be a little more polite," I said. "Doesn't Miss Manners cover that somewhere?"

"She says a good hostess always makes her guests feel comfortable," Ellen said. "Especially if they brought the food."

Ellen and Adam had come bearing pizza, antipasto, and Chianti after I called Ellen to tell her the latest development. Adam had blandly assumed we were back on speaking terms, and since he had the pizza, I decided to be forgiving.

"Well, what does make you think it wasn't suicide?" Adam asked. "Did you tell Frank?"

I shook my head. "That's the trouble, you see. I don't know what bothers me. I feel like the deductive cells in my brain are all asleep, and the intuitive ones are trying to do all the work. Frank doesn't take intuition very seriously."

"And he calls himself a detective!" Ellen said.

"Why would someone kill Sharon?" Adam asked. "From what I hear, she was pretty decent."

"Ingle!" Ellen said. "My favorite candidate. I knew he was a villain."

"Hold the phone," Adam said. "Do you have any reason to suspect Ingle, other than personal dislike, that is?"

She waved away his objections. "When we talked to him, and to Sharon, too, each of them made some nasty remarks about the other."

"So they weren't good friends," Adam said. "That's a pretty weak motive for murder."

"What if Sharon knew who killed Duchat?" I asked.

"She'd have told the police," Donald said finally.

"Maybe she just found out," I said. "Maybe she didn't know for sure, and she wanted to talk to the person first."

Donald looked skeptical. "She thought someone was a murderer, so she called him for a private chat about it?"

"You're right, Donald," Ellen said, smirking at me. "No one in her right mind would set up a tête-à-tête with a murder suspect."

"There's another thing," Donald said. "Could someone make you take enough sleeping pills to kill you? Without a struggle? Those were just over-the-counter stuff, so . . ."

"But we don't know what killed her," I said. "Not for sure. The pills could have been window dressing."

"The tapes," Traci said. "Is that a clue, Geneviève?"

We all looked at her.

"The Spanish tapes," she said. "I have been thinking, why was Sharon studying her tapes if she was killing herself? Does not that seem peculiar?"

"Maybe she just used them to distract herself," Ellen said. "You know, if she took sleeping pills or something, she might have wanted something to listen to, to keep from freaking out.''

"No.'' I shook my head. "Traci's right. That is one of the things that was wrong. She might put a music tape on, but a lesson tape? I don't think so.''

"But why would the killer put the tape on?'' Adam asked. "That doesn't make sense either.''

"To make it sound like Sharon was alive and well?'' I chewed at my finger. "Long enough to let the killer get away? Those tapes run for about an hour and a half. Omega said she called Sharon a little after one, and Sharon said she was with a client, right? And then Clint said he thought Sharon was at lunch when he got there, probably right after that, because her door was locked.''

They were gazing at me expectantly. Unfortunately, I had no idea where I was going with this.

"And?'' Ellen prompted.

"I don't know. I'm just talking to myself. It seems like that ought to mean something, but . . . Did Clint mention anything about hearing the tapes?''

"No.'' Traci shook her head. "If he had heard them, he would not think Sharon was out, *non?*''

"*Oui,*'' I said. "And when we got there the door was unlocked, and the tape was playing. So that means . . .'' I sighed. "Darned if I know.''

Everyone looked disappointed.

"And, of course, all of that presumes that Clint and Omega were telling the truth,'' Adam said. "If one of them is the killer . . .''

"Okay,'' Donald said, "but if they are telling the truth, it does mean something. Maybe that the killer was the client Sharon told Omega about.''

I smiled at him approvingly. "So maybe someone can find out who was there between one and two o'clock.''

"Victor Ingle,'' Ellen said. "I've said so all along.''

"You're becoming obsessed,'' I said. "If you had a con-

fession from someone else, signed and notarized, you'd still
. . . Oh, that's it!''

Four mouths fell open, eight eyebrows shot up, and a
chorus of unintelligible exclamations flailed me.

''The note,'' I said. ''The suicide note. That's what was
gnawing at me. There was a letter in the printer, about a
show the gallery was planning. I thought it was strange that
she was planning a show for August at the same time she
was killing herself.''

Adam scratched his head. ''Well, she could have written
the letter before she decided. Before she knew about the
ID bracelet.''

I nodded. ''That's what I thought. But the printer was
on, as if she had been using it.''

''Sure,'' Donald said. ''She wrote the—the note.''

''After she wrote the letter about the upcoming show?''

''Well, yeah.''

''So she took the show material out, wrote the suicide
note, and then put the show letter back in the printer?''

We all sat staring at one another in silence.

''Either that,'' I said at last, ''or she wrote the suicide
note and then the show letter.''

''Maybe she wrote the suicide note on another machine,'' Ellen said slowly.

''And then turned her printer on even though she wasn't
going to use it? Anyhow, there was no other machine in
the office, no typewriter, at least I didn't see one.''

Traci shook her head. ''There is no other one that I have
ever seen.''

''Or,'' I said, ''she wrote the suicide note somewhere
else, at home maybe, then brought it to the office, and that
still doesn't explain why she turned on her printer.''

''You're right,'' Adam said. ''There's something wrong
with every scenario.''

''The only thing that makes sense,'' I said, ''is that
someone else wrote the note and brought it along. The

printer was on because Sharon was using it to write her letters about the show she planned to be around for.''

''And someone killed her.'' Traci's voice quavered.

''And turned on the tape player,'' I said. ''Between two o'clock and when we got there at three-thirty.''

Ellen opened her mouth.

''Yes, yes,'' I said. ''We all know who your candidate is. But it still could have been Clint or Omega. Anyhow, figuring that out isn't our job.''

''Funny,'' Adam said. ''I could have sworn several of us mentioned that in the past. Not including you.''

I ignored him. ''Now, of course, comes the really difficult part.''

''Which is?''

''Telling all this to someone with a badge. Someone who, I very much fear, will be Frank Monroe. Call me hypersensitive, but I have this feeling that Frank doesn't welcome my help.''

''Oh, come now,'' Adam said. ''That's never stopped you before.''

''And we must tell this, Geneviève,'' Traci said earnestly. ''I think it is something important.''

It was. And so I called the station. God smiled upon me and allowed Frank Monroe to be gone for the day, since apparently even cops are allowed time to eat and sleep. It was only a reprieve, but I accepted it and left a message for him to call me in the morning. A message from me would be just what he needed to start his day right.

Chapter Twenty-seven

It was almost nine o'clock when our little detective agency closed for the night, leaving me to contemplate a peaceful recess. I decided I'd treat myself to a lengthy bubble bath, followed by the new Mary Higgins Clark novel, and a full night's sleep. I was on my way to the first of these pleasures when the phone rang.

It was Annie. "Sorry I couldn't get back to you sooner. I dug up the information about that art dealership, but I don't think it will help much."

"You never know," I said. "What did you find out?"

"Well, Paul Cataline did have a partner, Kevin Hunter. When the investigation into the thefts closed in, Hunter was the one accused of running the operation."

"I'll bet."

"Yeah, his name was on all the incriminating papers. But a lot of people thought he was set up. Kevin Hunter was, by all accounts, a nice guy who impressed everyone as being scrupulously honest. Smart, but naive. However, the evidence was pretty strong, and the art world was going through a bad round of thefts. So Hunter went to prison for a couple of years."

"And his partner?"

"Ah, his partner. Paul Cataline disappeared. There was nothing to incriminate him, but he blew town anyway, the rumor being that he went off to Europe."

"Where he became Mark Duchat." I sighed. "What happened to Kevin Hunter after he got out? You don't think he came looking for Duchat?"

"No, ma'am. He got out and found himself broke. Evidently Duchat didn't go away empty-handed. Hunter got a job in an art-supply house. His wife left him. People who knew him say he was pretty beaten down. Tried to locate his ex-partner, but no one believes he wanted revenge. He just hoped he could get some of the money back. Anyhow, about two years ago, he was killed in a hit-and-run accident. So he's not your killer, Mom. Poor guy."

I sighed. "Duchat didn't leave many friends, did he?"

"One other thing," Annie said. "Duchat was married at the time, to the sister of his partner, if you can imagine that. She was implicated in the thievery, too, but she got probation, for a year."

"Really? Where is she now?"

"I don't know. She went to stay with some relatives. She was pretty young, ten or twelve years younger than her brother—he was a stepbrother, I think. In fact, that was why he was so keen on getting the money from Duchat. He felt responsible for bringing her and Duchat together. He had looked after her since their parents died, when she was still in school. She inherited a fair sum from her mother, and when Duchat took off, he took little Sally Ann's money, too."

"Whoa," I said. "What was her name?"

"Sally Ann. Why?"

"Sally Cataline," I said. "S. C." I explained about the ID bracelet.

"Interesting," Annie said. "So I did good, eh, Ma?"

"Don't call me Ma. Yes, you did good."

I hung up and headed once more for a rendezvous with a tubful of bubbles, where I could contemplate the meaning of Annie's information. But before I reached my goal, I heard a tapping at my door. Great popularity was highly overrated, I decided, as I stalked across the room, flung open the door, and narrowly missed a punch in the nose.

"Oh, my!" Mrs. Shelby, her tiny fist aiming for another knock on my door, teetered, and I caught her in mid-plunge. She peered at me through her thick lenses. "Oh, Genny, I—I just wanted to see if you were all right. After Saturday. Mrs. Schofield, downstairs, she said no one was hurt, but sometimes Mrs. Schofield doesn't know what she's talking about. You know how she is."

I laughed. "Well, this time she's right, Mrs. Shelby."

"Well, good. I just couldn't believe anyone broke in here. Why, nothing like that has ever happened before. Now my son wants me to move. I said, well, Jack, burglars could be anywhere, after all. But he's having one of those chains put on my door, anyway."

"Well, that's not a bad idea," I said. "It certainly can't do any harm."

"I suppose. I was visiting my son, you know. I just came home this morning and Mrs. Schofield told me what happened. I'm so sorry I wasn't home, dear. If I'd been here, maybe the burglar wouldn't have broken in."

I had a vision of little old Mrs. Shelby confronting a possible murderer. "I'm just as glad you weren't here, Mrs. Shelby. You might have been hurt."

"Well, maybe." She didn't sound convinced. "It's too bad your friend didn't stay until you got home. I think these burglars find out if someone's . . ."

"Excuse me, Mrs. Shelby. What friend is that?"

"You know, just that she had to leave. Of course, she didn't know there would be a burglar . . ."

"Mrs. Shelby, dear, when was that?"

She squinted at me. "Why, on Saturday afternoon. I was waiting for my son to pick me up, and I thought I heard him in the hall. But when I opened my door, it wasn't Jack, it was your friend. I thought it was you at first, because she had a key, she was locking the door, and I said hello. But then I saw that she was taller, and I said, oh you aren't Genny. And she kind of jumped, I think because the elevator made that noise it does, and I said, that's just the elevator, my son is coming. And she said, well, I'm late, I'll see Genny later, and she went down the stairs."

Thank goodness for Jack Shelby's timely arrival, I thought. "What did she look like, Mrs. Shelby?" I asked, knowing as I spoke that it was a question not likely to bear fruit.

"Oh, Genny, I'm afraid I can't tell you much. My eyes aren't so good, you know. But, dear, you probably don't give many friends your key, so . . . Oh, my! Do you mean that maybe that woman was the burglar?"

"Well," I said, "I haven't given anyone a key."

"Oh, Genny, I'm so sorry. If I had just imagined—I could have sent Jack after her. All I can tell you is that she is taller than you—her head came up to the light fixture, you see. I think she had light-colored hair, I could just see a little bit of it because she was wearing a coat with a hood. Oh, I feel so foolish!"

It took a cup of tea and a lot of soothing before poor Mrs. Shelby stopped chiding herself, but at last she toddled off to her own apartment and I immersed my bemused self in the promised bubble bath, where I sat and allowed thoughts to chase themselves around my brain until the water was cold.

If my intruder was a woman, the field was narrowed to Sharon Cromwell and Omega Starlight. But Sharon was dead, so that left only . . . except that Sharon had been alive on Saturday, so it could still have been . . . but we knew she wasn't the murderer . . . unless she really had committed suicide? Impossible, I told myself. Well, at least improbable. So that meant Omega . . . or, of course, it meant that the person who was running around searching for whatever was not the murderer. As Frank Monroe had suggested. Curses!

Well, at any rate, I started again, the breaker-and-enterer was a woman, which meant Sharon or Omega.

Or.

I was beginning to hate these sudden jogs in my thought processes. Ah, well! Or, consider one other female possibility: Sally Ann Cataline. Or maybe Sally Ann Hunter, if she went back to her maiden name, as most women surely would under the circumstances. However, I didn't know anyone by either name, no one who would know where I live.

Of course—I gave myself a mental slap—if the woman could track down Paul Cataline under a new name, it would hardly be a major feat to locate me.

Another possibility: Maybe Sally Ann had changed her name, which was certainly reasonable if she wanted to start a new life. Then she might now be someone who did know me. Omega, for example. Omega Starlight was surely a false name, and . . .

I flashed back to my sophomore Lit class. Talking about aliases, pseudonyms . . . Someone—Jean Ann?—saying something about . . . no, it was Denny, I thought, arguing that a criminal wouldn't choose an alias like Omega. She'd pick a nice, normal name.

A name like Mary Smith? A no-frills name for a decidedly no-frills young woman. Sharon Cromwell's assistant could have easily found out where I live.

Was this how paranoia began? My brain was beginning to feel as shriveled as my fingers, so I ended both the bath and the conjectures. It was time to admit that I was not a detective, I told myself. In the morning I would drop all of this in Frank Monroe's lap. For now, I would get into bed, read some favorite poetry. "The Marshes of Glynn" and maybe some Gerard Manley Hopkins. Fill my mind with "Pied Beauty" and "The Windhover" instead of murder.

It didn't work as well as I'd hoped, but eventually I did settle down and go to sleep.

And found myself suddenly awake in that twilight just before dawn, my heart hammering, clinging to the remnant of a dream. Nightmare, perhaps. I tried to remember it, but only bits and pieces remained. A dark-cloaked figure following me through a maze of hallways. I kept ducking through doors, locking them behind me. But my pursuer had keys for every door. He—she?—kept coming, got within arm's length again and again, but each time I narrowly escaped. Until—until the last time—I felt my arm clutched, turned to look at my captor—and woke with a jolt.

Not an unusual reaction, I reminded myself. But there was something about that last second. What had I seen? I struggled with it for several minutes and finally gave up, punched my pillow, and willed myself to go back to sleep.

And remembered. What I had seen in that last second was the face of—Sister Madonna. Sister Madonna, saying, "It's simple logic, Mrs. Galway!"

Oh, great! Some breakthrough that was! Moreover, the last hope of sleep fled. After lying there cursing the darkness for another five minutes or so, I got up and headed for the kitchen to make coffee.

Brian used to say we all knew more than we realized we knew. The trouble was, he said, the brain doesn't have a good filing system, so finding the right pieces of knowledge wasn't easy.

So all right. If I couldn't sleep, maybe it was because my subconscious was trying to cough up whatever it was that was stuck in there. If I got my questions down in black and white, maybe something would get jarred loose.

I got a notebook, poured a mug of coffee, sat down at the kitchen table, and invited inspiration.

Okay, start with the new fact: it was a woman who had used my key to get in. What might I know about her?

The fact that she was taller than I was no help; that would be just about every adult except Traci. She had my key, which meant she was surely the intruder at St. Phil's. She knew who I was, otherwise the key wouldn't have done her any good. Still fit either Sharon or Omega. Or Sally Ann, whoever she was. Any one of them might have been searching for whatever would incriminate her.

Then, why did she go to the trouble of returning my keys? She didn't take any pains to conceal her search of Duchat's place, or Traci's. Except—wait. She didn't have a key for Duchat's; she had to break in. Did have a key for Traci's, and maybe she'd have covered her tracks there if Traci hadn't come home too soon. Question: Why would she care if I knew she broke in, since anyone could have stolen the keys at school that night? Because she didn't want the school break-in connected to the other break-ins and the murder? Or maybe because she didn't want us to know she hadn't found what she was looking for?

Another thought: Where did she get a key for Traci's apartment? Traci insisted she hadn't lost a key, and her spare was on a hook in her kitchen, right where she left it.

I sighed. I kept coming back to questions about those stupid keys. And the feeling that I knew the answers, if I could just locate them among all the clutter.

And, of course, it didn't matter anyhow, if the ubiquitous searcher had been Sharon. A little breaking and entering wasn't much to worry about compared to murder.

So much for digging about in one's subconscious, I concluded. What you found was a bunch of random thoughts connected by threads that defied untangling.

A halfhearted sun hoisted itself up into the branches of the maple tree and peered into the kitchen, and I went to get ready for the day. Frank Monroe would be calling, and I would just have to hope that he was more adept at untangling threads than I was.

Chapter Twenty-eight

St. Philomena's was settling down on Wednesday. Sharon Cromwell's death was a topic of conversation, of course, especially among the seniors who had exhibited work at her gallery. But it was as if her death had moved the whole affair a step away from the school and its denizens. The meager information available to the media as yet strongly suggested suicide, which added to the general assumption that everything was now resolved.

Donald, Traci, Ellen, and I did nothing to upset the assumption. First, because we had no desire at all to spend another school day quelling semi-hysterical adolescents, and second because Frank Monroe had been rather emphatic about his desire to keep our theories out of the general body of knowledge. He had said so when he returned my call that morning, his wary greeting turning to cautious interest over the news that my intruder was a woman, and then to downright warmth when he heard about the new S. C.

"Believe it or not," he said, "we were playing with the problem of the letter in the printer already. Every once in a while we do notice something, Gen. But the news about Duchat's having a wife with the initials S. C. is interesting."

I was about to utter a modest acknowledgment of his gratitude, but he continued.

"Of course, no one got around to mentioning that Duchat had a partner in a previous business, let alone a wife. That kind of slows us down, you see. It'd be kind of nice to be able to take those little shortcuts enjoyed by you folks who tell each other secrets and forget to tell us.''

I reminded myself to never willingly acquire a video phone, which would have given Frank the satisfaction of seeing my face aflame. As it was, he had to content himself with my meek and sniveling voice offering apologies.

''Okay,'' he said. ''I'm getting used to it. Do you think you could do one thing that might help us for a change?''

I assured him that I would do anything and everything, that my one wish in life was to be of service to my country and my police force.

There was a faint but unmistakable snort from his end of the line, then, ''It'd be a real good idea to keep this quiet for a bit. Including all the speculations your detective committee came up with yesterday. Give us a chance to work on the information, and maybe no one else will get killed in the meantime. So if you guys will just keep it to yourselves . . .''

''We can do that,'' I said. ''Roger. Wilco. Ten-four.''

''Right,'' he said, and hung up.

I had waylaid Traci and Ellen in the school parking lot to give them the message, and Ellen went to relay it to Donald. Therefore, the school was lulled into relative peace.

Life was ready to go on. We had our spring play, *Arsenic and Old Lace*, to get under rehearsal. Sister Mary Grace and I were codirectors, and she was down with a cold, so I had the first read-through that night all to myself. I stopped at the office before lunch to borrow the master key that would let us in and out of the auditorium and prop room.

''How terrible about Miss Cromwell,'' Sister Madonna said. ''That poor woman must have felt so overwhelmed with guilt.''

''Um, yes,'' I said, feeling a little guilty for not letting Madonna in on the rest of the story. On the other hand, I couldn't imagine why she would feel better thinking Sharon had been murdered. In fact, she might feel worse, considering that it meant there was still a murderer among us, one who had now killed twice.

"The police do believe Miss Cromwell committed suicide, don't they?" Was it my guilty conscience that made me feel she was looking at me suspiciously?

I have never been able to lie to a nun, even when I really wanted to, as in tenth grade, when Sister Magdalene asked me if I'd been smoking behind the bleachers at the Central-Newman game, and I knew the penalty was writing a thousand-word essay on the evils of tobacco.

I closed the door so that I could break my promise to Frank privately. Actually, I only bent it a bit, in that I didn't share the particulars, just that certain circumstances made the police suspect foul play, and that we had been asked not to spread the news around.

"I see," Sister said when I had finished. "Well, I understand why the police want to keep the information to themselves for a while. If someone was indeed desperate enough to murder a second time, it would be better that he think he's succeeded in ending the investigation. If he thought someone knew something . . ."

I nodded. "It wouldn't bother him—or her—much to add number three."

"Mrs. Galway, please be very careful, won't you? All of you, Miss Beaupré and Mr. Tomcyk as well."

I gave her my heartfelt assurance on that score and left the office.

Adam was coming down the hall. He looked surprised at seeing me, although I couldn't imagine why, since I belonged there. My own surprise was far more appropriate.

"Fancy meeting you here," I said.

He grinned. "Didn't expect you to be sent to the office. What did you do?"

"Got sassy with a teacher," I said. "Let that be a warning to you."

"I get along great with teachers," he said. "Sister Madonna called us to come in and go over specs for the new computers. They sent me, because my reputation with teachers is spectacular.''

"Is it now?"

"And to prove it, I'll buy you dinner tonight."

"I'll let you." Suddenly I realized that the hallful of plaid skirts and blue blazers seemed unusually quiet, and I could almost hear ears flapping. "Later," I murmured, and went down the hall to the lounge, wearing my most severe face.

In the lounge the talk was all about Sharon's suicide. Traci, Ellen, Donald, and I sat at one table, afraid to join in lest we let slip something we were supposed to keep secret. It was a relief when the others left a few minutes early.

Once out of danger of being overheard, I remembered my brainstorming of the night before, and asked Traci if she knew whether Omega Starlight was an assumed name.

She looked puzzled. "I do not know, Geneviève. Why do you ask?"

I hesitated, and Ellen gave me a suspicious look. I hadn't told them about Annie's call, or Mrs. Shelby's visit. Did Frank intend for me to keep that to myself, or could I share it with the people who, after all, were in on everything else?

"What are you up to?" Ellen asked.

"I'm not up to anything. I just—well, I was thinking that maybe there's someone else with the initials S. C."

"And why were you thinking that?"

I sighed. "I don't know. Just curious."

Traci looked doubtful. "I will see what I can find out. I do know some people who have known Omega for a long time. Perhaps they will know."

"Thanks," I said. "And—um—what do you know about Mary Smith?"

"Not very much," Traci said. "Why . . . Oh, you do not think Mary could be the S. C. person?"

"What in heaven's name put that poor soul on your list?" Ellen asked. "Honestly, Gen . . ."

"I was just asking," I said. "It just seemed as if it's the kind of name that could be false."

Ellen clucked. "I see. How does the saying go? Every Tom, Dick, and Harry is named Mary Smith? And then, after acquiring a name she hoped would assure anonymity, she sent the bracelet to identify herself. You must write a logic text someday, Gen. You could revolutionize the science."

Donald and Traci laughed. It's easy to amuse young people.

"I will see what I can learn, Geneviève," Traci said, giving my hand a comforting pat.

The door opened and Sarah came in. "Tea for Sister Madonna," she said. "And for her guest, Mr. Sowinski." She grinned at me. "They certainly are getting along well."

"Well, that settles it," Ellen said. "Might as well line up the caterer and the florist. I wonder if Mr. Merryman would give you away?"

"I wonder if one might hope to have a private life?" I asked, suspecting that my face was much pinker than I would have liked. I gathered my purse and my dignity and departed, ignoring the snickers behind me.

For a change, we had an uninterrupted afternoon of classes, after which I met with the drama club for their first read-through of the play. Following the week and a half of turmoil we had been through, it felt wonderful to be involved in normal activities again, and I was determined to keep all thoughts of murder at bay for the rest of the day. I drove home with my car radio tuned to the "Music of Your Life" station, and sang along at full volume. There was a fuzz of green along the hedges, and a host of crocuses nodded at me as I turned into the driveway.

And there was a red MG at the curb.

Okay, I thought. *Enough, darn you.*

I pulled into my parking space, took my big, heavy flashlight out of the glove compartment, and got out of the car. I stomped around to the front of the house, up the steps, and across the porch. I yanked the door open and strode toward the stairs.

The door to Mrs. Schofield's apartment flew open. I jumped and almost dropped my flashlight as I spun around.

"Hi, Mrs. Galway!" It was Mrs. Schofield's granddaughter. "Oh, I'm sorry, did I scare you?"

I gulped. "Well, Melanie! Nice to see you again."

"Did you see my new wheels? Radical, isn't it?"

"Your new . . . ?"

I peered through the oval glass as she pointed.

"Ah—the red—that's yours?"

She laughed. "Mine and the bank's. Got it just last week. I'll be paying for it until I'm Gran's age. But I thought, what the heck? I'm too young to have good sense, right?"

"Absolutely right," I agreed, laughing along with her, hoping that the laughter wasn't going to turn hysterical. "It's a great car. Enjoy it."

In seconds she was gone and I trudged up the stairs and let myself in. I collapsed on the sofa and pulled a pillow over my face. I wondered if there might be a prize for jumping to conclusions.

After a while I finished enumerating the ways in which I was an idiot and went to take a quick shower and change clothes. Adam would be coming by in less than an hour. I decided I wouldn't mention this little episode to him. Nor my speculations about Omega. Or Mary Smith. Or anything else remotely connected with detective work.

From now on I would be Genevieve Galway, English teacher. Period.

Chapter Twenty-nine

"I have found out what Omega's true name is," Traci said. "It is Darlene Kormann. I am sorry, Geneviève."

I poured a cup of coffee and sat down at the table with Traci and Ellen. "Thanks anyway," I said, "but don't worry about it." It was a beautiful morning, sunshine poured into the faculty lounge, and I was enjoying the start of my new life as a retired detective.

"I do not yet know about Mary Smith," she said. "No one knows her very well."

"It doesn't matter," I said. "I'm sure the police will find out anything that's needed to solve the case."

"What!" Ellen stared at me. "When did you reach that conclusion?"

"I have every confidence in our police force," I said. "As for me, I am quite content in my career as an English teacher. A very rewarding career."

"Oh, la!" Traci said, gazing at me in wonder.

"Something happened," Ellen said. "I'll find out sooner or later."

Bernadette came in, giving me the opportunity to change the subject. The school day started and I went forth, virtuous in my firm resolve. It was an uneventful day, just as I had planned.

The girls were gathered in little groups, playbooks in hand, when I got to the auditorium after my last class. Sarah was in the hallway, giving Mr. Merryman a message from Sister Madonna.

"Well, if that's what Sister wants, that's what she'll

get.'' He made it sound like a threat. ''I hope she knows that varnish is expensive, is all. But it's no skin off my nose.'' He scowled at Sarah, who made ingratiating noises. ''Them halls is going to get scuffed no matter what, all that traffic.'' Shaking his head, he turned and stomped down the hall, and Sarah scuttled back toward the office.

Sister Madonna fought a valiant though losing battle to keep St. Phil's old floors gleaming. Not a paper clip fell to our floors that didn't cast a shadow.

I gulped. Not even a paper clip.

''Mr. Merryman!'' I hurried after him, past the last of the girls closing their lockers and hastening toward freedom.

He turned and waited, his eyebrows at half mast.

''Do you remember—ah—you found my keys yesterday?''

He growled.

''I just—ah—where did you find them? If you remember, that is. I mean . . .''

''Of course I remember. I ain't senile, Miz Galway. Why wouldn't I remember? I remember I told you where I found them keys, too. Outside 103. I ain't the one has trouble remembering.''

''Oh, yes. I know. I meant—well, where exactly were they?'' He drew himself up, ready to pounce, and I hurried to clarify. ''Well, I mean, were they on the floor? By the door, I mean? Or, maybe, behind the water fountain? Or . . .'' My voice failed me.

''Miz Galway, what did I tell you? Did I say them keys was behind the fountain? No, I said they was beside the door, didn't I? That means on the floor, don't it? Not behind nothing, not hanging on the wall, not floating around in the air somewheres.'' Shaking his head, he turned and stalked away.

I stood there, rerunning the scene from Friday night as I stared at Sister Madonna's shining hallway. Lights illuminating every inch, myself following the cops down the hall, past Traci's room.

I trudged back to the auditorium and sat in front of the stage, trying to listen to the girls' run-through, hearing instead my brain cells weaving the threads I had been spinning the night before. Smoothing out the tangles, adding the last strands, the obvious ones that had been tantalizing me since Monday. There was just one more to find, and I was sure it was working its way to the surface.

I wished I didn't know what I thought I knew.

"Mrs. Galway?"

The voice seemed to come from my right shoulder, making me jump. Rita was standing beside me, and the look in her eye suggested that this was not her first attempt to reach me.

"Don't you think so?" she asked sternly. Behind her, Lucy looked mutinous.

"Oh, I . . . well . . . hmmm," I mumbled.

"But, Mrs. Galway," Lucy said, "that sword looks stupid. It isn't like a cavalry saber at all."

"Well, we don't have a cavalry saber," Rita said. "And Teddy is supposed to be crazy, so . . ."

"Not about Teddy Roosevelt, he isn't. He thinks he is Roosevelt. He'd know if he had the right weapon."

I sighed. "I'm sorry, girls. I just . . . I have something else on my mind right now. I really do apologize. Let's call it a day, and tomorrow we'll work it out. Okay?"

"It's because of all this other stuff, isn't it?" Rita shook her head. "It is kind of weird, going on just like always. I mean, you don't have murders and suicides happening every day."

"Thank heaven," I said. "And we do need to go on just like always. It's just that I've been trying to think of something I ought to remember but don't. It's distracting."

"Oh, yes," Lucy said. "I know what you mean. Like someone asks you who did a certain song, and it drives you crazy till you remember."

"Exactly," I said. "Anyhow, it's almost five o'clock now. Time for all of us to get home and get some dinner."

We gathered up the props, including the sword that annoyed Lucy. I had to agree that it wouldn't pass muster with any knowledgeable Rough Rider; it was the sword we had used last year for *Joan of Arc*. I put it back with St. Joan's shield and helmet, promised to locate a more authentic weapon, locked the door of the prop room, and led my flock to the back door.

The March wind slapped us as I opened the door.

"Oh, wow!" Lucy said, as her long hair whipped across her face. "By the time I get to the bus, I'll look like Cinderella's ugly stepsister!"

And the last little thread zinged into place. The last thing I hadn't known I knew. A hard little knot of regret settled in my stomach. If it hadn't been for Sharon, I might have decided not to clinch that last piece that would complete the puzzle. Duchat, I would bet, was an accident, a combination of anger and fear. But poor Sharon—she was a sacrifice, and she hadn't deserved to be.

I let the last of the girls out, and stood by the door for a few minutes willing myself to get on with it. Finally I went down the hallway, my footsteps echoing softly in the empty school. I unlocked Sister Madonna's office and went in, closing the door behind me. The light was fading, leaving the room in shadow, and I turned on the lights and moved reluctantly to the computer.

I knew the password because Sister Charlotte and I had set up the files last year, and in seconds I was in. And in not much more than that, I had realized that the file I wanted wasn't there. I went back and checked again. No luck.

There would be backup files, of course. To get those, I'd have to call Sister Madonna. I debated waiting until morning, which would at least allow the poor woman to have dinner and a decent night's sleep before I hit her with a new disaster. However, that would mean that I wouldn't get a decent night's sleep. On balance, it seemed best to get it over with.

I picked up the phone and punched the convent's number. Sister Pat answered.

"Hi," I said. "This is Genevieve Galway. Is Sister Madonna available?"

I waited while she went in search, listening to the silence.

A silence that was broken by the smallest of clicks, so small that I couldn't be sure I heard it.

Chapter Thirty

Sister Madonna said, "Hello, Mrs. Galway?" just as a firmer click came, the sound of a door latch opening.

I half turned, watching the door open, and said to the phone, "Uh, hello?"

"Yes, Mrs. Galway? What is it?"

"Hang up," Sarah said softly.

"Oh," I said. "Sarah. Hi. I was just . . ."

"Hang up," she said again, still softly, but this time reinforcing her request by pointing a small gun at me.

Somewhere I had heard that one should make no sudden moves at such times. I put the receiver down very carefully. "Sarah," I said, smiling pleasantly, I hoped. "What in the world are you doing with a gun?" Even a stupid question, I thought, might serve to keep communication alive.

"You should have let well enough alone," she said. "I never wanted to hurt you."

"Well, of course," I said. "Why would you?"

She looked sad. "We have to go over to the auditorium," she said. "Come on."

"Wait," I said. "Are you going to shoot me, Sarah?"

"Not unless I have to." Her lips tightened. "Let's go."

"Oh, Sarah," I said, "why don't we just stay here? We can talk, can't we? If you'd just put down the gun . . ."

"No." She shook her head. "Not here. We'll talk over at the auditorium. Come on." She sounded a little testy. Another rule from whatever book on criminal behavior I had been reading: Do what they tell you to do.

I moved slowly and carefully to the door and walked in front of Sarah and her gun down the hall to the auditorium.

"Oh," I said. "It's locked. And my keys are in my purse, in the office. Why don't we . . . ?"

"Use my key," she said, tossing it to me. "Hurry up."

Fumble as I would, eventually the door was unlocked and we went in. Sarah waved me on to the prop room.

"You know," I said, "Mr. Merryman will be coming back, Sarah. The Parents' Club meets tonight."

"He won't be here for two hours yet," she said. "That gives us plenty of time."

"Time for what? You did say you weren't planning to shoot me, Sarah, isn't that right?'

"I don't want to." She sighed. "I never wanted to hurt anyone. All I wanted was what was mine. What Paul took from me, and from Kev."

Keep them talking, right? Or was that what hostage negotiators did? Or people in movies? At any rate, since I seemed to have no other options that I cared to think about, it was worth trying.

"No one would blame you for that, Sarah. Duchat treated your brother badly, and I suppose . . ."

She frowned at me. "How did you find out about that? Never mind, it doesn't matter. Paul set Kevin up to take the blame. Kevin didn't know anything about it. He was such a good guy, so honest and . . ." She stopped, pressing her lips together.

"And he went to prison," I said. "And Duchat got away."

She nodded. "And took everything of Kevin's, everything of mine."

"How did you find him again?"

"I never wanted to see him again! I tried to forget all about him. After my probation was over, I went back to Chicago and went to secretarial school. I wanted Kevin to come back, too, after he got out of prison. But he had such an obsession about finding Paul, and he thought sooner or later he'd be back in New York. Kevin blamed himself for my losing everything. He gave me the job in their company, doing office work. I was just out of high school, and I was going to go to college. But when I met Paul—oh, he was so wonderful!'' She laughed, a short, bitter sound. ''Anyhow, Kevin kept trying to track Paul down. Found out he went to Europe. Then, just about the time he finally found out Paul was back in this country, with a new name, he . . .''

I had been inching backward while she talked, her eyes gazing at a spot over my head. Her eyes focused on me again, and I stopped.

''They said Kev's death was an accident,'' she said, ''but I knew who did it. I just knew.''

''Well, I understand how you must have felt. . . .'' I said.

''I followed him here,'' she said. ''I sent him the bracelet he had given me, so he'd know. I wanted to talk to him, that's all. I wanted him to give me the money he stole. It was the least he could do.''

''Absolutely.''

''He ignored me. And then, when I saw him at the art show, he laughed at me. When he went back to the office, I went after him. He was threatening Traci about something. I heard her say, 'Let me go, you're hurting me,' and then she ran out.''

She sighed again. ''I went in. He was standing there, holding her scarf, and he looked furious. I asked him again to do the right thing for a change.''

She stared at me, remembered anger in her eyes. ''He always had all the answers! He thought he was smarter than anyone else. He glared at me and said, 'You were stupid then, and you're still stupid,' and he turned away. I was so angry! Before I knew what I was doing, I picked up that statue and . . .'' She stopped, shaking her head.

''Sarah,'' I said, ''you didn't mean to kill him. You can explain . . .''

''I didn't mean to do a lot of things,'' she said. ''I wasn't going to hurt you the other night. I just wanted to find my bracelet, and whatever records Paul had that might mention me. And money. I was sure he'd have money there; he always used to do business for cash when he had the dealership in New York. He told me then that it was for special circumstances, and I shouldn't worry about it." She snorted. "I always believed what he told me. Anyhow, there was nothing in his apartment. Except his gun. It was lucky that I decided to take that, wasn't it?"

"Mmm," I said.

"So then I figured maybe the bracelet was in the package he left at Traci's. But I couldn't find anything in her apartment, either. So I came to school to look in her classroom. And when I saw you, I figured you had the same idea. I just wanted to get whatever you had found."

"I hadn't found anything," I said.

"No," she said, "but you still wouldn't let it go. You had to go back to Paul's apartment. If you had just stayed out of it . . ."

"I know," I said. "I'm sorry. But what you did can be explained, Sarah. You don't need to kill me."

"You're forgetting Sharon," she said.

I hadn't, actually, but I had hoped Sarah would.

"Um," I said, edging back another inch or two, "what do you mean, Sarah?"

She made an impatient gesture. "Oh, I heard you talking to Sister. You just couldn't let it alone, could you? Everyone would have believed it was suicide."

"The police know it isn't," I said, but she ignored me.

"She was a nice woman," Sarah said, sounding sad. "I didn't want to hurt her. But they had to stop looking for someone else with the initials on the bracelet."

"But they won't," I said. "Sarah, sooner or later . . ."

"She didn't suffer, anyhow," Sarah said. "I put the medicine in her coffee, and she went to sleep. She didn't even know when I put the plastic over her face."

"Listen, Sarah," I said, "there are extenuating circumstances. You were under a lot of stress."

"We need to go over by the shelves," she said, pointing with her gun.

"Oh? Why is that, Sarah?"

She smiled. "That unit is unsafe, you know. You should look at it, Gen. It could easily fall on one of the girls. I mentioned it to Mr. Merryman tonight, as he was leaving. I told him how you noticed it. He's going to see to it in the morning. Or maybe even tonight, during the Parents' Club meeting."

"Ah," I said.

"Let's go and look at it now," she suggested. "You'll see how, if it tipped over just as you were reaching for something on the top shelf, it would come down right on top of you. It could kill you."

"Really," I murmured.

"Yes," she said. "One of the legs is just ready to collapse. Go and look at it."

"Well," I said, "I'll take your word for it, Sarah. If it's all the same to you, I believe I'll let you shoot me instead. I'd hate for everyone to think I died in a silly accident. Under the circumstances."

A frown flickered across her face.

"Now, Sarah," I said, "this won't work. I'm not the only one who figured out that Sharon didn't commit suicide, you know. The police will still keep looking for—"

"They won't be looking for me. You're the only one who knows about Paul and me. I heard you talking about Omega's name, yesterday, in the lounge. They didn't know why you wanted to find out. And if you'd been sure, you wouldn't have been sneaking around trying to get into the personnel records, you'd have told the police."

"The police won't believe this was an accident," I said. "They'll start wondering who could have got in here. There aren't that many people with keys. And I don't think they'll suspect Sister Madonna. Or even Mr. Merryman, who re-

ally has no reason to kill me when it's so much more fun
to terrorize me.''

"Accidents happen all the time," she said impatiently.
"So do coincidences. You had Sister Madonna's keys. I
don't have any more time to talk, Gen. Let's get this over
with.''

I took two steps backward and came up against a table.
A helmet fell over with a metallic clank, and Sarah's head
jerked toward the sound, long enough to let me snatch St.
Joan's sword and swing it as hard as I could against her
arm.

The gun clattered to the floor, and I thwacked her again,
hitting her shoulder. The plastic blade snapped, and Sarah
sprang at me and yanked my arm behind my back. I kicked
at her, connecting with an ankle and throwing her off balance, but I was clearly outmatched. Even with a bruised
arm, Sarah had the advantage of five inches and fifteen
pounds on me, not to mention she was twenty years
younger. Slowly but surely she pushed me toward the
shelves.

There is one advantage to small stature, however. I had
learned it from my infant daughters, who were innocent of
evil intentions, but effective nonetheless. I bowed my head,
then brought it up and back with all the force I could muster, right under Sarah's chin. It was very painful.

Fortunately, it was equally painful for her, as I had good
reason to know.

"Unghh!" she said, staggering slightly and losing her
grip on my arm. I scooted to the side and ran toward the
door, but Sarah recovered and lunged at me, her face filled
with fury. I gathered all the force I had left into a desperate
shove. Sarah went sprawling backward, and I seized the
opportunity to do an end run.

Not quite fast enough, though. Sarah's tumble had
landed her within reach of her gun. I flung myself behind
a wardrobe trunk as she got to her knees and raised the
gun.

And suddenly the backdrop for *Brigadoon* began sliding past us, the casters squeaking ever so slightly. Sarah's mouth fell open as the heather on the hill flowed by.

From behind the far side, Sister Madonna said, "Now, Miss Joplin, stop this immediately!"

Sarah whirled around, waving her gun. She never saw Sister Pat gliding up with a large polystyrene boulder.

Sister Madonna stood looking down at the unconscious form. "Patricia, I do hope you didn't hit her too hard."

Sister Pat sniffed.

"Well," I said, "it took you ladies long enough."

"I'm sorry, Mrs. Galway." Sister Madonna smiled soothingly. "But you know, it was very hard to hear you. We couldn't make out where you were going. Sister Charlotte said it was the gymnasium. Sister Pat said the auditorium, but then when we got there, no one was there. Then we heard a noise from the prop room. And here we are. It was very clever of you to leave the receiver off the hook."

"Actually, I thought you'd call the police, Sister. You could have been killed, you know."

"Sister Charlotte has called the police, of course. I'm sure they'll be here momentarily. But there was no time to lose, Mrs. Galway. We had to act."

I was certainly in no position to argue.

Chapter Thirty-one

The police had come and asked their questions, and had gone away, taking Sarah along. Mr. Merryman had returned to open up for the Parents' Club, and had expressed his thoughts about all these goings-on. Parents were arriving, drifting into the music room, casting curious glances at me. Possibly they were wondering why one of their daughters' teachers was wearing a blouse with the sleeve half torn out, a large, rapidly coloring bruise on her cheek, a cut on her chin, and a hairdo that might be more commonly seen on MTV.

Neither Sister Madonna nor I was interested in satisfying their curiosity at the moment. I was not used to the rigors of hand-to-hand combat, and my thoughts were dwelling on the prospect of a warm bubble bath, a cup of hot amaretto tea, and a stereo playing Chopin.

Sister Madonna shooed me into her office and locked the door behind us.

"Soon they'll all be in the music room, busy with their meeting," she said. "Then we can escape. I just don't feel up to giving an explanation tonight."

"Amen," I said fervently.

She sighed, settling into her chair and motioning me to another. "This has been a dreadful two weeks! Poor Miss Joplin—I am having a hard time believing she could do such things."

"Well," I said, "it just got away from her. Mark Duchat really brought her life crashing around her. I don't think the money would have driven her so hard, but she blamed him for her brother's death. Who knows, maybe she was right. Even then, she didn't intend to kill him. Then one thing just led to another.''

''If she had just come to me after Mr. Duchat's death,'' Sister said. ''We might have been able to help. But now there's Miss Cromwell's murder. And there was almost your own.'' She shuddered. ''How did you know Miss Joplin was the culprit, anyhow?''

''The keys,'' I said. ''When Mr. Merryman found my keys on Monday morning, I knew something was wrong. I just got sidetracked, and couldn't put it together.''

Sister shook her head. ''I'm afraid I'm still not putting it together.''

''Well, someone had used the key to get into my apartment, someone who obviously didn't want me to know. The only reason I could see for that was that she didn't want us to associate the school intruder with the other break-ins, hence the murder. So she brought the keys back.''

''But I don't see why that should have led you to Miss Joplin, Mrs. Galway.''

''Because Mr. Merryman found the keys first thing Monday morning. So someone had to bring them in during the weekend. But to do that, she'd have to have a key to get into the building. The only ones who had keys to get into the building were you, Mr. Merryman, and Sarah.''

Sister Madonna frowned. ''I should have thought of that, too. Where in the world was my mind?''

''Busy with many things,'' I said. ''The first clue should have been the intruder last Friday night. No sign of forced entry. But we just assumed it was someone who was lurking in the building before everyone left. I wish I'd kept concentrating on the uneasy feeling I had about those stupid keys. If I had, maybe Sharon Cromwell would still be alive.''

''Oh, my dear, you mustn't blame yourself for that. It ought to have occurred to many of us. But there was so much turmoil, I suppose we weren't as logical as we might have been."

"There were other things I should have picked up on, too," I said. "I think I just didn't want to know what was right under my nose. Traci's purse was mislaid at school, long enough for someone to get a copy made of her key. And she had mentioned that she'd be out that evening. We talked about the books Duchat had left at her apartment, and about Sharon's coffee habit. Sarah was always here when we talked about anything to do with the case."

"Well, there was no reason you should have thought about that, Mrs. Galway. Sarah was just—one of us."

"But I even saw her coming back to school around two-thirty the day Sharon Cromwell was murdered, and I still didn't let myself know. Even last night." I told her about Annie's call. "I had all the pieces then. I knew Sally was a nickname for Sarah. And I knew Sarah's middle name was Ann; I noticed it when we entered the records last year, because it's my daughter's name. Even then, I told myself Sarah's last name was Joplin, not Hunter, and I let it slip right past me when Annie said Sally was Kevin's stepsister. I just didn't know I knew. I didn't want to put it together, I guess. Didn't want anyone I like to be a killer."

"Not surprising," Sister said. "But why were you calling me, Mrs. Galway?"

"I decided to check Sarah's personnel file. Where she had worked, when. Any holes in the record. I was still hoping I was wrong about it. But Sarah's file had been erased. So I was going to ask you to get me the backup. I think Sarah was waiting for me to come out, maybe at my car. When the girls had all left and I didn't, she must have gotten anxious about what I was up to."

Sister Madonna sighed. "You were very fortunate, my dear. We owe a prayer of thanksgiving. And many prayers for Miss Joplin."

"Amen to both," I said.

She hesitated for a moment. "Oh, my. I know it's Lent,

but under the circumstances, I don't think the Lord would object to one small indulgence." She opened the bottom drawer of her desk and rummaged under papers.

My jaw dropped. Not that *I* would mind a stiff belt myself at this point, but Sister Madonna?

She came up smiling in triumph, brandishing two Snickers bars. "I thought there were a couple left!" she said, tossing one to me.

"Ah, ambrosia!" I said, ripping the wrapper and inhaling the aroma. "Sister, I would never have pegged you for a closet chocoholic."

She took a bite and smiled. "It's shameful, I know, to hide treats like this. Sister Agnes Marie is so determined to watch over our diets, she would be quite cross with me. But man does not live by carrots and broccoli alone, Mrs. Galway."

"You'll get no argument from me." I felt the chocolate coursing through my veins.

"My brother sends them to me," Sister Madonna said. "Every month. And for special holidays, he sends..." —she leaned toward me, her eyes sparkling— "... Cadbury!"

"No!" I said. "Not—not with almonds?"

She nodded. "He's a good brother," she said.

We sat and munched, taking small bites, making it last. Finally she sighed again. "Mr. Sowinski seems to be a very nice man," she said.

"He is," I said. "A very nice man."

She smiled at me. "It's been two years, Mrs. Galway."

"Sister, it's unfair to take advantage of a person who's under the influence of chocolate."

"I know," she said, laughing. "But, you know, it isn't good to be alone."

"Why, Sister Madonna, that's strange coming from you," I said.

"Oh, my dear," she said, "that's quite different. I'm not alone at all. You know, when you're called to do a particular task, you must do it. Even if it means you may give up another choice that you perhaps intended.''

''I guess,'' I said. ''But I'm not ready to make another choice yet, Sister. Maybe someday.''

''That's all right then,'' she said. ''You just think about it, though. As the song said, a good man is hard to find.''

''I'll keep it in mind,'' I said.